Robert Palmer Howard

Semi-Centennial Celebration

Introductory Address: A Sketch of the Life of the Late G.W. Campbell

Robert Palmer Howard

Semi-Centennial Celebration
Introductory Address: A Sketch of the Life of the Late G.W. Campbell

ISBN/EAN: 9783337415716

Printed in Europe, USA, Canada, Australia, Japan

Cover: Foto ©Andreas Hilbeck / pixelio.de

More available books at **www.hansebooks.com**

MEDICAL FACULTY, McGILL COLLEGE.

Semi-Centennial Celebration.

INTRODUCTORY ADDRESS:

A Sketch of the Life of the late Dr. G. W. Campbell,

and a Summary of the Early History of the Faculty,

BY

R. P. HOWARD, M. D.,

Dean of the Faculty.

REPORT OF SPEECHES

At the Banquet, Windsor Hotel, Oct. 5th, 1882.

Montreal:

GAZETTE PRINTING COMPANY.

1882.

THE INTRODUCTORY ADDRESS OF THE FIFTIETH SESSION OF THE MEDICAL FACULTY OF McGILL UNIVERSITY.

BEING A SKETCH OF THE HISTORY OF THE FACULTY AND OF THE LIFE OF THE LATE DEAN, G. W. CAMPBELL, A.M., M.D., LL.D.

BY R. P. HOWARD, M.D., L.R.C.S.E.,

Professor of Theory and Practice of Medicine, and Dean of the Medical Faculty.

GENTLEMEN,—We celebrate to-day the 50th session of the Medical Faculty of McGill University, an important period in the life of an individual, and in these days of unceasing activity and progress, a suitable stopping-place even in the history of an institution, affording an opportunity and suggesting the propriety of repeating the story of its beginning, glancing at the work it has done, and sketching the life of one just taken from us who was the last of the little band who either gave it an existence or established its early reputation.

The corner-stone of the present Montreal General Hospital was laid on the 6th June, 1821, and it was opened in the following May for the reception of patients. Doubtless, the possession of the hospital suggested to its medical attendants the idea of establishing a medical school in connection with it, and thereby, not only securing greater care and skill in the treatment of the sick, but providing for the performance of another function of an hospital, not sufficiently thought of by philanthropists—the practical teaching of the medical art. Equal to the responsibilities of their office as physicians to a hospital recently provided by the liberality of their fellow-citizens, and alive to the importance of affording Canadian youths, at least, the elements of a medical education at home, Drs. Stephenson, Robertson, Holmes, Caldwell and Loedel, five of the hospital staff, established the first Canadian Medical School under the name of the " Montreal Medical Institution," and its first course of lectures was given in the academic year 1824-25. The success of the undertaking was foreshadowed by the attendance of 25 students during its first session, not one of whom now survive. However, of its second session, Dr. Alfred Andrews of this city ; of its third, Dr. Hamilton Jessup of Prescott and Dr. Joshua Chamberlain of Frelighsburgh ; of its fourth, Dr. Abbott of Hochelaga ; and of its fifth, Dr. James B. Johnston of Sherbrooke, are still living.

The lecture-room was in a small wooden building in the Place d'Armes, where the Montreal Bank now stands. The branches then taught were : Principles and Practice of Medicine, by Dr. Caldwell ; Surgery, Anatomy and Physiology, by Dr. Stephenson ; Midwifery and the Diseases of Women and Children, by Dr. Robertson ; Chemistry, Pharmacy and Materia Medica, by Dr. Holmes. It was originally intended that Dr. Loedel should have taught Materia Medica, but for reasons now unknown, neither he nor his immediate successor, Dr. Lyons, appears to have given lectures in the Institution.

It is deserving of mention, that of the founders of the first medical school in Canada, one, Dr. Stephenson, was a native Canadian, and another was educated in Canada, having come to this country when only four years of age ; and from that time to the present, the Medical Faculty of this University, into which, as you will presently learn, the Montreal Medical Institution passed, has been largely composed of native Canadians. Indeed, at this moment, every member of this Faculty but one is by birth a Canadian, and, what is more significant, with the same single exception, every member of it received his medical degree in course at this University before he went to Europe to erect a superstructure upon the broad foundation which the authorities of McGill College at an early period in its history wisely insisted upon. Who shall say that our *Alma Mater* has not had confidence in her sons ? Who can fairly allege that Canadians have not realized their responsibilities to their country, or have proved recreant to her claims upon them ?

The next event in the history of the early days of this Faculty is of no little interest. As early as the year 1811, the Hon. James McGill, one of those noble-minded men who, having by their industry and ability realized a moderate fortune, feel it to be a privilege, if not an obligation, to give a portion of their means for the benefit of the country in which they have acquired their wealth, died, and bequeathed a valuable property and £10,000 currency for the purpose of endowing a college which was to bear his name, and form part of the University which he, in common with his fellow-citizens, believed it was the intention of His Majesty George III. to establish in Montreal.

I know not whether it is a necessary outcome of so-called popular or representative governments like those of Great Britain and the United States that provision for the establishment of institutions for the higher education of the people appears not to be a function of the Government, but a privilege, a duty assigned to private individuals. However this may be, notwithstanding the announcement made by the Lieut.-Governor of the Province to the Legislative Assembly in 1801 that it was the intention of His Majesty " that a suitable proportion of the lands of the Crown should be set apart " for the instruction of the people, and notwithstanding the establishing of " the Royal Institution for the Advancement of Learning," no grants of land were given, and were it not for the munificence of a private citizen, it is highly probable that an university for the education of the English-speaking people of this Province would not now exist, and certainly it would not have attained its 50th session. Relying on the good intentions of the government and upon the bequests of Mr. McGill, the Royal Institution, in 1820, obtained a Royal charter for " McGill College," but, owing to litigation as to the will, could not get possession of the estate bequeathed by that gentleman till 1829. It was a condition of the bequest that lectures should be given within a certain term of years ; but one year of that period then remained, altogether too limited a time in which to select and appoint among the then small population of Canada suitable persons to constitute a Faculty of Arts, the ratification of such appointments, moreover, requiring to be made by His Majesty. What was to be done ? The governors of the College communicated with the members of the Medical Institution with the view of constituting it a Faculty of the College, and in the minutes of the first meeting of the governors, held

4

on the 29th June, 1829, for the promulgation of the charter, the following entry appears :—

" After the public business was over, the governors of the Corporation
" held an interview with the members of the Montreal Medical Institution
" who had been requested to attend the meeting for that purpose. Owing
" to this interview, it was resolved by the governors of the Corporation
" that the members of the Montreal Medical Institution (Dr. Caldwell,
" Dr. Stephenson, Dr. Robertson and Dr. Holmes) be engrafted upon the
" College as its Medical Faculty, it being understood and agreed upon be-
" tween the said contracting parties that, until the powers of the charter
" would be altered, one of their number only should be University Pro-
" fessor and the others Lecturers. That they should immediately enter
" upon the duties of their respective offices. All of which arrangements
" were agreed to."

The first session of the Medical Faculty of McGill College was held in 1829–30, at which 35 students attended ; of whom survive our esteemed friends Dr. David, Dean of the Medical Faculty of Bishop's College ; and Dr. Johnston, of Sherbrooke. Of the third session, Dr. Macdonald, of Cornwall ; of the fourth, Dr. Joseph Workman, ex-Professor of Midwifery of the Toronto School of Medicine, and Dr. F. W. Hart, of St. Martinville, Louisiana, are also happily alive, and the former present to-day. The Faculty has continued its lectures annually ever since, ex- cept during the three years comprised between 1836-39, so that the present is its 50th session. It no longer, however, is entrusted with the management of the farm, a duty assigned it by the governors in 1833 ; which farm, by the way, is now covered by the University buildings, the several handsome structures belong- ing to Colleges affiliated with the University, the magnificent Museum in which we are now assembled, the recent gift of a private citizen, and not by any means his first act of munificence to the University, and the mansions which have been built on the streets extending south to St. Catherine Street, and from Uni- versity Street east to McGill College Avenue west. It is due to the memory of the first governors and promoters of McGill College to state here that they purposed to provide not alone for the teaching of Arts, but also of Divinity and Medicine, and that on the 4th December, 1823, five professors were appointed to the following chairs: Divinity, Moral Philosophy and the

5

learned languages, History and Civil Law, Mathematics and Natural Philosophy, and Medicine. The gentleman who had the honour of being appointed the first professor of medicine to McGill was Dr. Thomas Fargues, a graduate of Edinburgh and a resident of Quebec. However, it does not appear that he ever lectured; the contestation of the will prevented the institution from going into actual operation* for some years subsequently.

Turning now to the four men who were the founders of medical teaching in Canada, with but one of them was the speaker acquainted, and some who are present will, he feels sure, endorse what he is about to say respecting him. Dr. Andrew Fernando Holmes was born in Cadiz; the vessel in which his parents were sailing to Canada having been captured by a French frigate and taken to that place. He arrived in this country when but four years old; at 15 he became a student of Dr. Arnoldi, père, and subsequently graduated in Edinburgh in 1819, the subject of his thesis being "De Tetano." It was dedicated with filial affection to his father, and with gratitude to his former patron: "Danieti Arnoldi, armigero, chirurgo peritissimo, cujus sub auspiciis primum arti medicæ incubuit; hoc tentamen grati animi exiguum testimonium dedicat auctor."

Having returned from Paris, where he completed his studies, to this country, we find him, in 1821, elected an attending physician of the Montreal General Hospital, and, in 1824, taking an active part in founding the first Canadian Medical School. In that institution, and afterwards in McGill University, he lectured upon Materia Medica and Chemistry until 1835, when Dr. Archibald Hall divided with him the teaching of the former subject, while he continued the latter unaided up to 1844. That year, owing to the death of Dr. Robertson, he succeeded to the chair of the Theory and Practice of Medicine, and ably filled it up to the time of his decease. During the last eight years of his life he held the honourable position of Dean of the Medical Faculty, and to his studious care the College is mainly indebted for its valuable medical library, which for many years was kept at his private residence. Having sat under him as a pupil, and

* See the Canadian Magazine, Vol. IV, p. 172.

having enjoyed the privilege of his friendship as a colleague, I
can testify to the care and thoroughness with which he prepared
his lectures upon medicine, a characteristic of all the work he
ever undertook ; to the affectionate interest he manifested in the
welfare of the students ; and to the earnestness and constancy
with which he devoted his time, influence and means to the service of his God. He died instantaneously of fatty degeneration
of the heart, on the 9th October, 1860, while writing a notice
to convene a meeting of the Medical Faculty. A sketch of his
life has been written by his colleague, the late Dr. Hall.

Another person who played a conspicuous part in the early
history of our school, and perhaps even more in that of the University itself, was Dr. John Stephenson, a native of this city.
His father, of the same name, a merchant from Scotland, began
business in Canada the year after the conquest of Quebec—his
family being one of the three first English-speaking families who
settled in this city. Dr. Stephenson's education began at " Le
College de Montreal," where his diligence and love of study
won for him the regard of the Reverend Fathers. He afterwards
became a student in the University of Edinburgh, where he obtained the degree of M.D. in 1820, the title of his thesis being
" *De Velosynthesis.*"

It would appear from the records of the Montreal General
Hospital that most probably to Doctor Stephenson belongs the
honour of originating the Medical Institution, for in the minutes
of the meeting of governors of the hospital, under date August
6th, 1822, this entry is found : " That Dr. Stephenson be allowed
to put in his advertisement for lectures next winter that they
will be given at the Montreal General Hospital." That his
example bore fruit is shown by the minutes of the meeting of the
4th February, 1823, where it is noted that the medical board
of the hospital communicated to the governors its intention " to
deliver lectures on the different branches of the profession."
So great was the earnestness of young Stephenson in the cause
of education, and so much did he deplore the absence of any
provision for the proper education of the English-speaking people
of the Province, that his nephew, William Whiteford, Esq., of the

Temple, in a short notice of his uncle kindly written for me, and to which I am indebted for many of the facts herein stated, observes that he "was the first to begin the agitation which resulted finally in wresting from the hands of the heirs of Mr. James McGill the bequest of that gentleman towards a college"; but, "except from his own profession, he received very little sympathy." That the University is largely indebted to its Medical Faculty as a whole, and to Dr. Stephenson in particular, for the recovery of the bequest made to it by its founder, is further rendered probable by the fact that at a meeting of the governors of the College, held on 29th July, 1833, it was " resolved that the Medical Faculty of the College be authorized to use the means necessary to forward the interests of the College in the suit now pending touching the £10,000 bequeathed by the late Hon. James McGill," etc. At the same meeting Dr. Stephenson was nominated Registrar to the University. I have been informed by a reliable person (Dr. Joseph Workman) that the successful issue of the contest and the recovery of the estate was largely due to the untiring energy and personal influence of Dr. Stephenson. And this opinion is borne out by the testimony of the late Hon. Peter McGill, who, in some letters of introduction given many years ago to Mr. Whiteford, speaks of his uncle (Dr. S.) " as the man, of all others, to whom we owe the existence of McGill College." He did good work also as a teacher in the two institutions with whose foundation he was so intimately connected, having lectured upon anatomy and surgery from 1824 to 1835, and subsequently upon anatomy only up to the year of his decease, 1842. He is said to have been an able and eloquent lecturer, and was a man of considerable culture and great industry. For many years he had a large share of the confidence of the public as a practitioner, and until the time of his death his name was a household word amongst all nationalities in this city.

Dr. Wm. Robertson, the first lecturer upon Midwifery and the Diseases of Women and Children in the Institution, was descended from an ancient and respectable family in Perthshire, being the second son of the late James Robertson, Esq., of Kendrochot.

Of his early history I have only been able to learn that he studied medicine in Edinburgh, where he passed his examinations with credit. Almost immediately after he joined the 49th Regiment as assistant surgeon, at Cape Breton Island, in 1806, was subsequently promoted to the 41st as surgeon, served through the war of 1812, was present at the storming of Fort Niagara, and, on the declaration of peace in 1815, settled in this city and practiced his profession for nearly twenty-eight years. His ability, culture and social disposition secured him a large practice amongst the *elite* of the city. On the death of Dr. Caldwell, he was appointed to the chair of Medicine, which he filled until removed by death on the 18th July, 1844. His lectures are said to have been carefully prepared and slowly delivered ; but he was unable to instruct his pupils in the practice of the obstetrical art, for the University Lying-in Hospital was not established until November, 1843. In an obituary notice of Dr. Robertson by the editors of the Montreal *Medical Gazette* of 1st August, 1844, the following occurs : " He was gifted with great powers of intellect, which were much increased by an indefatiguable industry and an assiduous culture rarely equalled."

Of Dr. William Caldwell, the first lecturer in this school upon the Principles and Practice of Medicine, I have been unable to learn much. He was born in Ayrshire, Scotland, in 1782, and studied medicine and graduated in Edinburgh in 18 . He was surgeon to the 13th Regiment of Dragoons, and served in the Peninsular war on Lord Aylmer's staff. Dr. David, his private pupil, informs me that he was a man of severe military bearing, but of mild and amiable disposition—cool in judgment, wise in council, and kind in the treatment of his patients. His lectures on Medicine were scientific, and ably delivered from carefully written notes. He died on 23rd January, 1833, at the age of 48 years, of typhus fever, complicated with pulmonary gangrene. For many years he was a leading practitioner in this city.

It does not appear that any change was made in the *personnel* of the Medical Institution when it became the Medical Faculty of McGill College ; its lecturers became the lecturers of the

College, teaching the same subjects that they had taught previously, and in the same building.

On the death of Dr. Caldwell in 1833, Dr. Racey, a native of Quebec, and a young man of considerable talent, who had received his early training in the Montreal Medical Institution, and had completed his professional education at Edinburgh, the then British Athens for medical learning and teaching, was appointed associate lecturer on Midwifery (and perhaps on Surgery, Dr. Hall).

It was in the year 1835 that the man whose loss as a faculty we this day deplore, and whose life we are presently about to glance at, became officially connected with this University. That year some important changes were made in the teaching staff of the University. To Dr. Campbell was entrusted the chair of surgery, previously held by Dr. Stephenson, and that of midwifery, which had just become vacant by the removal of Dr. Racey to Quebec. Dr. Stephenson was thus enabled to devote all his time to the subject of anatomy ; and the labours of Dr. Holmes were reduced by the appointment of Dr. Archibald Hall associate lecturer with him on Materia Medica, while he continued alone responsible for the teaching of Chemistry.

The next important event deserving of mention was the establishing of the University Lying-in Hospital in the session of 1843–44, which provided the means of giving practical instruction in a very important branch of medical knowledge. The Faculty is deeply indebted to the kind co-operation of the many ladies who have watched over that institution since it was opened. It was in the year 1845 that the corporation of the University, at the suggestion of the Medical Faculty, took the wise resolve to extend the curriculum of study and to appoint lecturers upon Clinical Medicine and Surgery, the Institutes of Medicine, and Medical Jurisprudence. The first teachers of those subjects were respectively the late Dr. James Crawford, Dr. Robert L. MacDonnell, and Dr. William Fraser. By this step not only was there a means provided of imparting instruction in all the departments of medical study then deemed necessary in the best European schools, but an importance was given to clinical teaching and study, which has had the happiest effect upon the young men trained in the McGill School of Medicine. In assigning the duty of teaching at the bedside to one person, and making him responsible for the work, instead of leaving it to the several members of the medical staff of the Hospital indifferently, as it might chance to please them, efficient and regular bedside instruction was secured, to the great advantage of the students. Changes have been made from time to time in the system of clinical teaching pursued in this University till it has reached its present excellence, which I do not hesitate to say is unsurpassed in any hospital in the mother country, and not equalled in any in this. In 1849 the clinical chair was divided, Dr. Crawford retaining clinical medicine and Dr. MacDonnell taking charge of clinical surgery ; in 1870 a practical examination at the bedside by the professors of clinical medicine and clinical surgery was made a compulsory requirement for the medical degree ; and in 1874, twelve months instruction in clinical medicine and the same in clinical surgery were required, instead of six as before.

The new departure made by the Faculty in 1845 seems to have inaugurated a series of changes extending to the present, and all intended to elevate the standard of medical education and provide for the more thorough training of the student in the science and the art of medicine. As early as 1848 the corporation passed a statute rendering four years of professional study a necessary qualification for the medical degree of the University, although it did not require that the whole period should be spent in attending a medical school. At present, however, it is the rare exception for one of our graduates not to have pursued his studies for four winter sessions. In that same year botany was placed on the list of compulsory subjects.

An event of no uncommon importance to the University as a whole, and to its Medical Faculty as well, transpired in 1855, viz., the appointment of the present Principal to the charge of the University. His previous experience as the Superintendent of Education in his native Province and his enthusiasm in the cause of education, his energy and force of character, his familiarity with the genius and the wants of the people, his faculty of enlisting the interest and sympathies of those about him in whatever work he undertakes, his mature judgment, great attainments, and personal character have not only, as it were, galvanized into active life and vigour the previously struggling department of Arts, but have extended the proportions of the College to those of a great University, in which Faculties of Law and of Applied Science have been added to the original Faculties of Arts and Medicine ; and with which six independent colleges have become affiliated. The same fostering care has been extended by the Principal to the Medical Faculty. He has upon all occasions taken a warm interest in our concerns, assisted us by his wise counsel and experience, and strengthened us by his personal sympathy and support. And we are very largely indebted to him for the possession of the fine building in which our Faculty has its present habitation. Even in a hasty glance at the history of a single Faculty of the University, it would have been an unpardonable omission not to pay a tribute to a man who, at a most important era in the life of the University, revived a general interest and zeal which had well nigh expired ; evoked a spirit of liberality amongst the citizens ; inaugurated and organized a comprehensive system of higher education adapted to the wants of a new country, yet not inferior in its intrinsic value to the systems of older countries ; collected a body of competent teachers imbued, in some measure at least, with the lofty aims and devotion which characterize himself ; won by his rare qualities the confidence of the people, the regard and co-operation of his colleagues, the admiration and respect of the students ; and infused into every department of the University his own vitalizing, energizing spirit. The name of John William Dawson must ever rank alongside that of James McGill as the co-founder of this great University.

Time will not permit me to trace step by step the improvements which have been made in the teaching capabilities of our medical school, and a hasty allusion to some of them must suffice. One of the most important was the establishing, in 1876, of a three months summer session, during which short courses of lectures upon special subjects have been given partly by the professors and partly by instructors appointed for that purpose. In this way the attention of the classes has been directed to topics which cannot well receive sufficient consideration during the winter sessions,—such as the diseases of women and children; diseases of the eye, ear, throat and skin; operative and minor surgery; the urine; symptomatology; electro-therapeutics; the art of prescribing, etc. Clinical instruction is also regularly given during the summer months by two of the professors in the General Hospital; and the practical instruction of senior students in gynæcology is continued in the University Dispensary, an institution opened by the Faculty in 1879 for that purpose and for the treatment of skin affections. Instruction in the employment of the microscope in medicine forms a special summer course, and was begun in 1875.

The establishing of this summer course makes the academic year in this school last nine months, and it is very gratifying to find that the number of students availing themselves of the advantages it offers is steadily increasing.

Another important advance was made in 1876, when the indefatigable Professor of Institutes began a series of weekly demonstrations in morbid anatomy.

While bedside teaching is on all hands admitted to be essential to the student of medicine as. a preparation for the practice of his art, the great value of the examination of the diseased body after death is not sufficiently recognized. It, and often only it, reveals the truth or error of the diagnoses formed. It, and only it, will sometimes account for an anomaly observed during life, or explain the failure of treatment observed by the most experienced. Nothing like it cures men of over-confidence—of hasty conclusions. Nothing more enlarges their view of the possibility of similar morbid processes producing dissimilar symptoms—and of identical alterations developing unlikeness, even contrarity, in their vital manifestations. I hope the time will come when enlightened people will, in the interest of their families, as well as of the public, request, not reluctantly consent to, a careful post-mortem examination of their deceased relatives, at least when anything of an unusual or obscure nature has appertained to the illness which has proved fatal.

In 1878, the University, recognizing the great value of a thorough knowledge of practical anatomy to the medical students, instituted an examination in that subject which must be passed in order to obtain the degree in medicine. Finally, in 1879, a physiological laboratory was added to the technique of the chair of Physiology, and the senior students have now the opportunity of studying practically the essentials in the chemistry of digestion, the secretions and the urine, and of following a demonstration course in experimental physiology with the use of apparatus.

Passing from this brief sketch of the history of our medical school and of its founders, we ask your attention to the notice of a man who, though not a founder, was a very early and successful builder up of the school, and for many years presided over its destinies as its Dean.

The late Geo. W. Campbell, A.M., M.D., LL.D., was born on the 19th October, 1810, in Rosencath, Dumbartonshire, Scotland. His father was factor to the Duke of Argyle, a Justice of the Peace and Deputy-Lieutenant for the County of Dumbarton, of which the Duke of Montrose was their Lord Lieutenant. Mr. Campbell, who lived in stirring times, was an able and energetic man, and took an active part in public matters. After a life of great integrity and irreproachable conduct, he died at the age of 82. His mother was a daughter of Donald Campbell, of Ardnacross, Mull, Argyleshire. She died, after having had a large family, at the early age of 42, beloved by all to whom she was known ; and it may be interesting to mention that she had four brothers, three of whom, after reaching the rank of captain, and distinguishing themselves highly, fell gloriously in the Peninsular War. By the death of his eldest brother, Dr. Campbell recently inherited a small entailed estate on the shores of Loch Long, in the same parish, and also became the representative of an old branch of his clan, his paternal grandfather having been the nearest male relative and heir to Sir Alexander Campbell of Arkinglass, by whom the entail of his estates was (perhaps naturally) broken, and his property divided between his two daughters.

Dr. Campbell received his early education from his dear old

friend, the Rev. Dr. Mathieson, who was tutor in his father's family for many years, and who will long be remembered here. During his undergraduate course at the Glasgow University he highly distinguished himself, and, after graduating in Arts, won and held the Brisbane Bursary of £50 stg. a year during the four years of his attendance on the medical classes. Then, having passed one session in Dublin, he obtained the degree of M.D. of Glasgow University, and proceding to Edinburgh, took the L.R.C.S. in 1832. In May of that year he came to Canada, and began immediately the practice of his profession. Notwithstanding his youth, for he was then but 23, he rapidly acquired the confidence of those who became acquainted with him, and, what better establishes the actual qualifications of the man was his selection by the founders of this school for the chairs of surgery and midwifery at the early age of 25. In the same year he was elected an attending physician and surgeon of the Montreal General Hospital, and it was in that institution that he acquired the surgical skill which tended not only to his own advancement, but made the Hospital the resort of patients from all parts of the Province, and, after a time, added very greatly to the reputation of McGill College as a surgical school—a reputation which has not suffered in the trusty hands of his successor, the present professor of surgery. After eighteen years service in the hospital he resigned, and was placed upon its consulting staff, but continued the remainder of his life to take an active interest in hospital work, attending regularly the consultations of its staff, and assisting them by his great experience and good judgment, and not unfrequently aiding them with his skilful hands, especially if the operator were experienced. He retained the lectureship upon midwifery till 1842, when he resigned in favour of his intimate friend, the late Dr. Michael McCullough. It was the same year in which the late Dr. O. T. Bruneau succeeded to the chair of anatomy, rendered vacant by the death of Dr. Stephenson. He now confined his teaching to his favourite subject, and for 40 years, from first to last, faithfully and ably lectured on the principles and practice of surgery, until declining health convinced him that it was his duty to resign. When it is remembered that during nearly the whole—certainly during three-fourths of that time—he had a very large general private practice, and for 18 years of it was an attending physician of the General Hospital, besides being on the boards of management of several public institutions, it will at once appear that he must have not only been a very diligent man, but must have had an ardent love of his profession, and felt a deep interest in teaching. Nor were his professional duties performed in a perfunctory manner. None of his colleagues were more regular in their attendance, and up to the last he kept himself acquainted with the progress of practical surgery. His love of that branch stimulated him to note the wonderful changes that have arisen in the practice of surgery of late years, and his sound judgment and surgical instinct enabled him very frequently to adopt at once what were real improvements and to reject what were spurious.

> " Not clinging to some ancient saw,
> Not mastered by some modern term,
> Not swift nor slow to change, but firm."

On the death of Dr. Holmes in 1860, Dr. Campbell was appointed Dean of the Medical Faculty, and the following resolution passed by that body indicates how he conducted himself in that and his other relations to the Faculty :—

" That the Medical Faculty of McGill University has heard with profound regret and sorrow of the unexpected death in Edinburgh of their beloved and respected Dean, the late Geo. W. Campbell, A.M., M.D., LL.D., Emeritus Professor of Surgery in the University. An active member of this Faculty since 1835, he contributed very greatly, by his distinguished abilities as a teacher of surgery, to establish the reputation of its medical school ; and as its Dean since 1860, by his administrative capacity, his devotion to the duties of his office, his wise counsels, his unvarying kindness and consideration for his colleagues, and his high personal character, he not only increased the efficiency of the department of the University over which he presided, but secured the cordial co-operation of all its members in the advancement of its interests, and attached them personally to him as their most valued friend and most distinguished and honourable colleague in the teaching and practice of the medical art.

" And, further, that this Faculty tenders to the bereaved family of their beloved Dean its deep-felt sympathy in the irreparable loss which has so unexpectedly befallen them, the profession to which he belonged, and the community in which he so long, so lovingly and so successfully laboured."

As a lecturer, he was clear and emphatic, making no attempt at oratorical display, nor affecting erudition. Devoid of mannerism, he tersely and in well chosen Saxon words dealt with the essential and the more important features of the subject he had in hand. In his lectures his own mental constitution, clear apprehension and practical mind led him to occupy himself chiefly with what is well established in surgical pathology, to sketch boldly, but faithfully, the symptoms of disease, and to insist emphatically, yet briefly and soundly, upon the proper method of treating it. Quite alive to the great extension of the curriculum of the modern medical student, and to the almost innumerable facts that he is expected to store away in his memory, and heartily sympathizing with him, he never indulged in unnecessary hypotheses and scrupulously avoided minute and trivial details, obsolete practises and equivocal speculations. He taught surgical anatomy and operative surgery with much ability, and his college course of lectures has always been highly prized by the members of his class, and largely contributed to build up the reputation of the medical school connected with this University. And high as the position he attained as a teacher was, it was surpassed by his reputation as a practitioner. Like most men residing in cities of the size of ours, he was a general practitioner. Having had the advantage of a medical and surgical training in the large hospitals of Dublin and Glasgow under such men as Buchanan, Macfarlane, Cusack, Colles, Stokes and Graves, having been, as already mentioned, for many years attached to the Montreal General Hospital, where every member of its staff took charge both of medical and surgical cases, and having for many years practised all branches of the profession in private, it is not to be wondered at that he was an able and successful practitioner of the medical art. Devoting but little time, at least during the earlier period of his career, to what is called " society," he spent his evenings very largely in studying the standard authors in medicine and surgery. He was a very competent diagnostician in the various affections of the heart, lungs and other viscera ; and his good judgment and long experience made him very successful in the treatment of disease generally. He was also an able accoucheur. But it was in surgery that he was pre-eminent. Lecturing upon that subject for so many years, having a great love for it, and endowed by nature with a quick eye, steady hand and firm nerve, he was specially qualified to be a good surgeon ; and so he was. There are few of the great operations in surgery that he has not performed. He was a skilful and successful lithotomist, yet frequently practised lithotrity in conformity with modern teaching.

Like many other able teachers and successful practitioners of the medical art, he did not contribute many papers to medical science—a fact in his case to be regretted, as his ability and experience would have justified him in expressing opinions upon debated questions, and his opportunities for observation must have supplied him with ample materials. He was, however, a man of action rather than of words. The following are the leading articles which he published in the local medical journals :—
" Aneurism of the Arteria Innominata and Arch of the Aorta. Ligature of the Common Carotid."—(*Brit. American Journal of Med. and Physical Science,* 1845.) " Case of Osteocephaloma of Humerus—Amputation at Shoulder Joint—Secondary Hœmorrhage from Axillary Artery arrested by Compression." (*Medical Chronicle,* 1854.) " Two cases of Intestinal Obstruction from Internal Strangulation, and one of Inflammation and Perforation of the Appendix Vermiformis." — (*Ib.* 1854.) " Ligature of the Gluteal Artery for Traumatic Aneurism."— (*Brit. American Journal.* 1863.) " Ligature of the External Iliac for Aneurism of the Common Femoral."—(*Canada Med. Journal,* 1865.) " Excision of Elbow in consequence of Dislocation of Head of Radius and formation of large Exostosis."— (*Ib.* 1868.) " Valedictory Address to Graduates in Medicine." (*Med. Chronicle,* 1859.) " Valedictory Address to Medical Graduates."—(*Canada Med. Journal,* 1867.) " Introductory Lecture at Opening of Session 1869-70 of Medical Faculty of McGill College."—(*Ib.* Vol. VI)

In what are called medical politics he took no very active part ; yet he at all times manifested much interest in any movement or measure intended to improve medical education or

2

advance the status of the profession, or protect its legitimate interests. As an influential member of the Medical Faculty of this University, and for many years as its Dean, he promptly entertained and advocated any proposal that promised to prove beneficial to the school as a teaching body, to the students, or to the medical profession and public. And it was in recognition of these services and of others rendered by him as a member of the corporation of this University to the cause of higher education that induced that body to honour itself by conferring on him the degree of LL.D.—*honoris causa.*

In whatever relation of life we regard the late Dr. Campbell, we shall find much to admire, and few men have as well deserved to be presented to medical students and medical men as an examplar for their imitation.

As a citizen, he took an active interest in almost every public enterprise calculated to develop the material interests of the city and the country generally, protect the health, and elevate the morals of the community. Thus for many years he was a Director in the Montreal Telegraph Company, the City Gas Company, the Bank of Montreal, of which last he lately was made Vice-President, and was a stockholder in these and many other mercantile ventures; such as Shipping, Insurance and Mining Companies, cotton, woollen and other manufactures. He took a live interest in procuring the appointment of a city health officer, and upon several occasions formed one of a deputation to the municipal authorities for such purposes as advocating general vaccination, erection of a small-pox hospital, passing of by-laws to improve the sanitary condition of the city, etc. Nor did he fail to assist with his personal influence and his means the various institutions in our midst intended to provide for the bodily wants and the moral and religious needs of the people.

As a medical adviser, he was not only eminently capable, but painstaking and warmly interested in his patients, and they recognized in him a judicious and sympathizing friend as well as a competent physician.

As a colleague he was held in the highest esteem for his professional attainments and skill, his straightforward and honourable behaviour, and his consideration for the feelings and reputation of his brethren. In cases of difficulty or responsibility, his opinion and aid were eagerly sought and as generously given, and many who hear me can testify to the sense of relief and the feeling of confidence his participation in a consultation at once produced. By nature and practice a gentleman, and familiar with the many difficulties which often embarrass the formation of a reliable opinion upon the nature and appropriate treatment of disease, he never intentionally spoke disparagingly of a rival practitioner, nor by inuendo weakened the confidence of a patient in his attendant : having satisfied his own mind by a thorough examination of a case in consultation, he frankly, but courteously, stated his opinion, and in the subsequent management of it, loyally and heartily co-operated with the medical attendant. The absence of petty jealousy and his readiness to acknowledge —nay, to eulogise—professional ability in others, made him the trusted and beloved teacher and colleague. If any evidence were needed to indicate the esteem in which he was held by the profession of which he was so distinguished a member, and by the public whom he so long and faithfully served, much might be adduced. Let it suffice to recall the public dinner given to him by his brethren on his return from Europe after his first visit to his native land. The chair was occupied by his much-esteemed friend the lamented Sutherland, who, with that good taste and felicity of expression of which he was so capable, made known his personal regard for his friend, and in most feeling and eulogistic terms declared the esteem in which he was held by the whole profession. The profession was largely represented at the dinner, and several of its representative men testified to the high professional and personal character of the man they had met to honour. Amongst the few kind and manly sentiments which his full heart permitted him to utter, one expression deserves recording, as it was the reflex of his own kind heart. He " felt proud to say that he believed he had not a personal enemy in the whole profession." The many resolutions of sympathy and condolence, of regret and respect, which were passed by the corporation and by the Medical Faculty of McGill University, by the Medico-

Chirurgical Society of Montreal, by the Medical Board of the Montreal General Hospital, by the College of Physicians and Surgeons representing the medical profession of the Province, and by the Canada Medical Association, representing the medical men of the Dominion, and those passed by the Board of Directors of the Bank of Montreal, of the Montreal Telegraph Company, and of the Montreal General Hospital, are further unmistakeable and spontaneous tributes to the worth of the departed one.

And were it quite proper to lift the veil of privacy and follow the departed into domestic life, we should still, in the friend, the husband and the father, find qualities which, while they would command our admiration and deepen our affection for the man, would arouse within us aspirations to become like him.

As a friend, he was unswerving—faithful in watching over the interests of those to whom he held that relation ; reticent and charitable respecting their faults, sympathetic in their troubles, and constant in his attentions and deeds of kindness.

I cannot venture to speak of him as a husband and father— of such relationships none less than one of kin must dare to speak. This much may be said : that it was in the domestic circle he found his highest enjoyment—it was there he chose to spend his leisure hours. His chivalrous devotion to his wife and daughters—his hearty participation in the amusements and duties of his son, made him the object of their undying affection—the loved one gone before, whom they desire to join.

Such was Campbell—such was our late beloved Dean. The announcement of his unexpected death produced a thrill of emotion throughout the entire community—a feeling that a public calamity had occurred was experienced by the Canadian people. This Faculty had lost its head ; the profession had lost its councillor ; the sick had lost their ablest physician ; the city had lost one of its most distinguished citizens. The words of Dr. J. Brown, when inscribing his " Locke and Sydenham " to his old master, Mr. Syme, may truthfully be applied to our departed teacher and Dean—" *Verax—capax, perspicax—sagax, efficax—tenax.*"

" Were a star quenched on high,
  For ever would its light,
Still travelling downward from the sky
  Shine on mortal sight.
So when a good man dies,
  For years beyond our ken,
The light he leaves behind him lies
  Upon the paths of men."

When reviewing the developmental history of our medical school, we have recorded a good deal of what it has done ; but another portion of its work remains to be spoken of, however briefly, viz., the number of its students and of its graduates. It appears from the records that about 2,000 students have received their medical education in whole or in part in this institution, and that 917 have obtained its degree in medicine. These numbers alone are fair evidence of a large amount of good work accomplished by the Medical Faculty of McGill University ; and the positions attained by many of her alumni, the high professional qualifications assigned to them wherever they have practiced their profession, and their general loyalty to those time-honoured and lofty principles by which the great physicians of the past have been animated in their dealings with one another and with the public, all indicate the quality of the instruction given and the abiding influence of the moral lessons imparted by their *Alma Mater.* Her Alumni are widely scattered over the Dominion of Canada—are present in goodly numbers in many of the States of the neighbouring Republic—not a few of them have obtained appointments in the army-service of the mother country—and a few are practising acceptably in that country. One of them, at present, has the distinguished honour of representing Her Gracious Majesty as the Lieut.-Governor of this Province, several of them have seats in the Legislative Assemblies of the Dominion and its Provinces, many of them are teachers in the various medical institutions of Canada, and the great majority of them are practising the medical art with credit and profit to themselves and with benefit to their patients.

On this side the Atlantic at least, the holder of the medical degree of this University is, by common consent, accepted as a person well qualified to discharge the duties of a medical practitioner ; and I have never met a man who thought lightly of its possession. Of the *future* of our medical school, time will not permit much to be said. That the same success which has attended its past will accompany its future, I have no doubt. The energy, industry and ability that characterized its founders have never been wanting in their successors. The participation in the spirit and knowledge of their time, and the aspiration to lead in medical education, which were conspicuous qualities in its first teachers, are not deficient in their followers. And some of us, who must soon fall out of the ranks, look forward with implicit confidence in the youthful energy, the proved ability, and the progressive spirit of our younger colleagues to maintain and to extend the reputation of the Medical Faculty of McGill College.

It should be—it must be—the aim of this Faculty not merely to keep up with sister and rival institutions, but, true to her past, to lead them all. To do this, however, will require the active co-operation of the friends of medical education, and some united and strenuous effort on the part of the members of our Faculty. The capabilities of our school are crippled, and our efforts to improve them are impeded by the want of means. We have no endowments, and receive no pecuniary assistance from the University. Had we a Faculty Fund of $50,000, the revenue it would yield could be applied to making some very much needed alterations of and additions to our buildings, and to extending our means of teaching in directions that would have remarkable results on our usefulness. Our present building is too small. We very much need increased accommodation for our library, now numbering 8,000 volumes—perhaps the largest medical library in Canada. A laboratory for the teaching of practical pharmacy is now regarded as a necessary appurtenance of a great medical school, yet we do not possess it. A room for the meetings of the Faculty, and in which the professors, after their lectures, could meet the students without interfering with the next lecturer, is very much needed. Our museum will, ere long, be too small, and extra apparatus for teaching purposes is needed in all the departments. Then there are, at least, two directions in which our system of medical teaching could be most profitably extended. The first of these is the appointment of capable junior men to undertake the elementary teaching of the primary students at the bedside, in small classes of ten or twelve, from day to day. The physical appliances and means of detecting and discriminating disease are now so numerous, that nothing short of teaching every student individually at the bedside how to apply them—just as we teach practical anatomy—can properly qualify them either for efficiently acting as clinical clerks in their final years, or for discharging their higher duties as practitioners after they have graduated. I should regard this as a very important improvement on the present system of medical training; but we want means with which to pay well qualified men for the considerable time that such instruction would occupy. The other direction in which the system of medical education at present in vogue pretty well all over the world, I believe, might be most profitably extended, is the institution of a chair of comparative pathology. It is beginning to be felt by advanced pathologists that that obscure and difficult department of medical science, the origin and causation of disease, cannot make satisfactory progress unless the genesis of disease is systematically studied in animals lower than man, and in the vegetable kingdom also. Not until science has ascertained the conditions under which the various forms of disease originate, and the processes of evolution and modification they undergo throughout the organic kingdom—not until the first departures from normal development, nutrition, repair and dissolution can be detected, can we hope to prevent disease, or to arrest its progress. Yet such is the God-like aim, the inspiring hope, of the modern physician. Taught by the experience of the past of the limits of his power in the cure of disease, he seeks to prevent its development and its propagation, and, failing these, to arrest its course, moderate its violence, and, as far as possible, re-establish health. The endowment of such a chair would place our school in advance of those of the mother country in that respect, and without an ample endowment, a person possessed of the necessary attainments could hardly be obtained.

Such, then, are some of the uses for which we want a Faculty Fund, and we venture to suggest to the friends of our late Dean, amongst whom he practised so long and so faithfully, that the creation of such a fund, to be called " The Campbell Memorial Fund," would be a graceful tribute to the memory and the worth of a good man and an able physician. On this, the jubilee session—the golden wedding year—of the Faculty of Medicine of McGill College, the creation of such a fund by the citizens of this metropolis would be a gratifying evidence that its career and its work have merited their approval.

NOTE.—It is not generally known that the members of the Medical Institution were appointed, in 1823, by His Excellency the Governor-in-Chief of the Province of Lower Canada, the Board of Medical Examiners for the District of Montreal, as the following copy of the commission will show :—

To WILLIAM ROBERTSON, ESQUIRE, WILLIAM CALDWELL, M.D., JOHN STEPHENSON, M.D., A. F. HOLMES, M.D., H. L. LOEDEL, ESQUIRE, and to all others whom these presents may concern.

Pursuant to an Act or Ordinance made, provided and passed in the twenty-eighth year of his late Majesty's reign, intituled "An Act or Ordinance to prevent persons practising Physic and Surgery within the Province of Quebec, or Midwifery in the towns of Quebec or Montreal, without Licence," I do hereby appoint you, or any three or more of you, the said William Robertson, William Caldwell, John Stephenson, A. F. Holmes, and H. L. Loedel, in some suitable or convenient place and manner, to examine and enquire into the knowledge of every such person as ought to have such certificate or licence as by the said Act or Ordinance is required for the uses and benefits therein mentioned. And know ye further that I, the said George, Earl of Dalhousie, do by these presents determine, revoke and make void all and singular the commissions heretofore granted and in force for the appointment of medical examiners for the said district of Montreal, and all matters and things therein contained, hereby declaring the same to be null and void, and of no effect.

Given under my hand and seal-at-arms, at the Castle of St. Louis, in the city of Quebec, in the said Province of Lower Canada, on the twenty-second day of February, in the year of our Lord one thousand eight hundred and twenty-three.

Signed,   DALHOUSIE, Governor.

By His Excellency's command
  MONTIZAMBERT,
    Acting Prov. Secretary.

REPORT OF SPEECHES

AT

BANQUET AT THE WINDSOR HOTEL,

October 5th, 1882.

SEMI-CENTENNIAL CELEBRATION OF THE MEDICAL FACULTY,

BANQUET AT THE WINDSOR HOTEL,

OCTOBER 5TH, 1882.

The members of the Medical Faculty of McGill University celebrated the opening of the fiftieth session of the College by a banquet in the Windsor Hotel on Thursday evening, October 5th. There were about two hundred guests present, including some of the most distinguished members of the medical profession, not only graduates of McGill, but also representatives from other medical institutions, besides members of other professions and leading business men of the city of Montreal.

The chair was occupied by Dr. Robert Palmer Howard, Dean of the Faculty, and on his right sat His Honor the Lieut.-Governor Dr. Robitaille, Dr. Workman, Mr. J. H. R. Molson, Mr. F. W. Thomas, Dr. Covernton, Dr. D'Orsonnens, Mr. James Stewart, Mr. Andrew Robertson, Dr. Trudel, Mr. Thomas Davidson, Prof. Johnson and Mr. Alex. Campbell ; and on his left Principal Dawson, C.M.G., Dr. J. R. Chadwick, Sheriff Chauveau, President Buckham, Hon. D. A. Smith, Principal Howe, Mr. Hugh McLennan, Dr. Rottot, Prof. J. Clark Murray, Mr. D. Morrice, Dr. Andrews, Rev. Dr. Jenkins, Mr. John Molson, Dr. F. W. Campbell, Mr. Justice Torrance, and Mr. R. A. Ramsay. The vice-chairs were occupied by Drs. Scott, McCallum, Girdwood, Ross, Osler, Roddick and Gardner.

The following is a list of the guests who were present:—

Dr. H. Howard, Dr. Godfrey, Dr. Proulx, Dr. Bergin, Dr. W. R. Sutherland, Dr. Brigham, Mr. J. S. Hall, Dr. Kollmeyer, Dr. J. M. Stevenson, Dr. G. Pringle, Dr. Boulter, Dr. A. C. Macdonnell, Dr. McKay, Dr. Drake, Dr.

Hingston, Dr. Scott, Dr. Leprohon, Prof. Kerr, Mr. Moat, Prof. Bovey, Dr. Mayrand, Dr. Christie, Dr. W. Wilson, Dr. Butler, Prof. Archibald, Dr. A. D. Stevens, Dr. Mount, Dr. Hamel, Dr. Gibson, sr., Dr. Grant, Mr. Thos. White, M.P., Mr. David Wishart, Dr. Gibson, jr., Dr. J. Bell, Dr. Gillis, Dr. Armstrong, Dr. F. Scott, Dr. R. L. Macdonnell, Dr. P. R. Young, Dr. And. Henderson, Dr. Wigle, Dr. Dowling, Dr. McGinnes, Dr. Arton, Dr. Munro, Dr. Greaves, Dr. H. L. Reddy, Dr. Cotton, Dr. T. A. Greer, Dr. Crothers, Dr. W. H. Burland, Dr. M. O. Ward, Dr. Brossard, Dr. Mattice, Dr. J. C. Cameron, Mr. J. R. Dougall, Dr. O'Brien, Dr. Harrington, Dr. Girdwood, Dr. R. T. E. McDonald, Dr. Shufelt, Dr. T. L. Brown, Dr. Derby, Dr. T. N. McLean, Dr. Fortier, Dr. D. C. McLaren, Dr. H. B. Small, Dr. A. A. Browne, Dr. F. Warren, Dr. Buller, Dr. H. P. Wright, Dr. J. Hays, Dr. Fisher, Dr. Stephen, Dr. Josephs, Dr. Lunam, Dr. W. T. Duncan, Dr. McCorkill, Dr. G. T. Ross, Dr. Rugg, Dr. T. W. Mills, Dr. Robert Howard, Mr. Campbell Lane, Dr. Greenwood, Dr Major, Dr. J. Stewart, Dr. Laramee, Dr. Ross, Dr. Gurd, Dr. Groves, Dr. McBain, Dr. Ewing, Dr. Marceau, Dr. W. F. Jackson, Dr. R. C. Young, Dr. Blackader, Dr. McConnell, Dr. C. R. Jones, Dr. Wagner, Dr. R. L. Powell, Prof. Moyse, Mr. J. S. McLennan, Dr. O'Callaghan, Dr. Guerin, Dr. L. D. Mignault, Dr. Hans Stevenson, Dr. J. A. McDonald, Dr. Molson, Dr. Pattee, Dr. Shepherd, Dr. J. J. Farley, Dr. Perry, Dr. O'Brian, Dr. McCormack, Dr. H. Hunt, Principal McEachran, Dr. Copeland, Dr. Osler, Dr. Gustin, Dr. H. LeR. Fuller, Dr. White, Dr. Finnie, Dr. Youker, Dr. Alloway, Dr. Pinet, Dr. Webb, Dr. Stimpson, Dr. Kennedy, Dr. Chipman, Dr. Field, Dr. Dickson, Dr. Wilkins, Prof. McLeod, Dr. Reed, Dr. N. H. Smith, Dr. Loux, Dr. Harkness, Dr. Rodger, Dr. J. Macfie, Dr. Perrigo, Dr. Harkin, Dr. Rinfret, Dr. R. A. D. King, Capt. Sheppard, Mr. And. McCulloch, Dr. Roddick, Dr. McCallum, Dr. Van Norman, Mr. John Stirling, Prof. Cornish, Mr. S. E. Dawson, Mr. A. Manson, Dr. J. McIntosh, Dr. Duhamel, Dr. Whitwell, Dr. A. Lyon, Dr. A. R. Fergusson, Dr. Battersby, Dr. Trenholme, Dr. P. Robertson, Dr. Allard, Dr. Lamarche, Dr. Bristol, Dr. Raymond, Dr. L. J. McMillan, Dr. Turgeon, Dr. H. A. Mignault, Dr. Chevalier, Dr. Leclair, Dr. Powers, Dr. Bessey, Dr. Richard, Dr. Fuller, Dr. Mongenais, Dr. Whyte, Dr. Longley, Dr. Brouse, Dr. Gardner, Dr. Walsh, Dr. Chagnon.

" ' Hem, boys / come, let's to dinner ; come, let's to dinner /
O, the days that we have seen / "—SHAKSPERE.

———

THE MEMBERS OF THE MEDICAL FACULTY

OF

McGILL UNIVERSITY

INVITE THEIR GRADUATES TO CELEBRATE THE

OPENING OF THE FIFTIETH SESSION OF THE COLLEGE,

At the Windsor Hotel,

MONTREAL, THURSDAY, OCTOBER 5TH, 1882.

—————————————

" On the table spread the cloth,
Let the knives be sharp and clean;
Pickles get and salad both,
Let them each be fresh and green.
With small beer, good ale and wine,
O, ye gods, how I shall dine."
SWIFT.

MENU.

" Lay on Macduff:
And damn'd be him that first cries,' Hold, enough.' "—SHAKSPERE.

HUITRES DE BLUE POINT SUR ÉCAILLES.

" It is unseasonable and unwholesome in all months that have not an R in their name
to eat an oyster.—BUTLER, 1599.

POTAGE.

" The next thing is the supping of spoone meat made of good broathe of flesh , for such
brothes are very kindly to man's nature, and inginder goode
bloode.—THE REGIMENT OF HEALTH, 1634.

TORTUE VERTS.   CONSOMME FLORENTINE.

" Thou lack'st a cup of Canary."—SHAKSPERE.

HORS D'ŒUVRES.

TIMBALE A LA PERIGOURTINE.

POISSON.

" Master, I marvel how the fishes live in the sea!"
" Why, as men do aland ; the great ones eat up the little ones."—SHAKSPERE.

SHEEP'S HEAD A LA CREVETTE—Concombres.

AIGUILLETTES DE BASS A LA JOINVILLE—Pommes de Terre a la Parisienne.

" Set a deep glass of Rhenish wine."—SHAKSPERE.

RELEVÉS.

NOIX DE TORTUE VERTE A LA HUSSARD—Tomates Farcies.

ENTRÉES.

" Pretty little tiny kickshaws."—SHAKSPERE.

FILLET DE PERDRIX A LA PERIGUEUX.

CROQUETTE DE RIS DE VEAU A LA PILAU.

FRICASSEE DE POULET A LA CHEVALIER.

ROTI.

" Innocent as is the sucking lamb."   *" What say you to a piece of beef and mustard ?"*
" 'Tis no matter for his swellings, nor his turkey cocks."—SHAKSPERE.

FILLET DE BŒUF.   DINDONNEAU.   JAMBON.

SELLE DE MOUTON.

" Of mighty ale a large quart."—CHAUCER.

SORBET.

PONCHE A LA ROMAINE.

" *For this, be sure to-night thou shalt have cramps.*"—SHAKSPERE.

GIBIER.

" *The Partridge, Robin Redbreast, Cocke of the Wood,*
The Pheasant, Heathcocke, Moorehen, all are good ;
So the wild Mallard, and green Plover too,
Eaten with wisdom, as we ought to doe."—THE REGIMENT OF HEALTH, 1634.

CANARD NOIR. PLUVIER. POULE DE PRAIRIE.

LÉGUMES.

" *Let the sky rain potatoes.*" " *I had rather have a handful or two of peas.*"
SHAKSPERE.

POMME DE TERRE. PETITS POIS VERTS. CHOU-FLEUR.

ASPERGES HARICOTS VERTS.

MAYONNAISE.

DE VOLAILE. DE HAMARD. DE LAITUE.

ENTREMETS.

" *Solid pudding against empty praise.*" " *Bless'd pudding,*
POPE. *The more thou damn'st it the more it burns.*"
SHAKSPERE.

POUDING AUX RAISINS SERRES—Sauce Eau-de-Vie.

PETITS FOURS MELES. GATEAUX ASSORTIS. CONFISERIE.

GELEE DE CHAMPAGNE AUX FRUITS. PATE A LA POMPADOUR.

GLACE A LA NAPOLITAINE.

DESSERT.

" *When we eat Peares, boldly we may drink wine ;*
Nuts against poison are a medicine ;
Peares eaten without wine are perilous,
Because raw Peares are venemous."—THE REGIMENT OF HEALTH, 1634.

FRUITS ASSORTIS.

" *Coffee which makes the politician wise.*"—POPE. " *Give me a cigar.*"—BYRON.
" *Run nothing but claret wine.*" " *Fetch me a quart of sack.*"—SHAKSPERE.

TOASTS.

THE QUEEN:

> " *Here's health to the Queen and a lasting peace:*
> *To faction an end, to wealth increase.*"—OLD SONG.

THE GOVERNOR-GENERAL:

> " *Genteel in personage, conduct and equipage,*
> *Noble by heritage.*"—CAREY.

LIEUTENANT-GOVERNOR OF QUEBEC:

> " *Of very reverend reputation, Sir,*
> *Of credit infinite, highly beloved.*"—SHAKSPERE.

THE PRINCIPAL OF THE UNIVERSITY:

> " *He was a scholar and a ripe and good one:*
> *Exceeding wise, fair spoken and persuading.*"

SISTER COLLEGES:

> " *A fellow feeling makes one wondrous kind.*"—GARRICK,

THE GRADUATES:

> " *Old friends, old times, old manners, old books, old wine,*"—GOLDSMITH.

SISTER PROFESSIONS:

> " *Temperance the best Physic, Patience the best Law, and Good Conscience*
> *the best Divinity.*"—SANDERSON.

THE FOUR FOUNDERS:

> " *There were giants in the earth in those days.*"

THE MONTREAL GENERAL HOSPITAL:

> " *A theme of honor and renown.*"—SHAKSPERE.

THE LADIES:

> " *Bibamus salutem earum et confusionem ad omnes bacularios.*"
>   DUFFERIN.

> " *Then to breakfast with what appetite you have.*"—SHAKSPERE.

THE CHAIRMAN called on Dr. Osler, Secretary of the Faculty, to read the letters he had received from invited guests.

From over four hundred letters of regret at not being able to be present, Dr. Osler referred to or read extracts from the following :—From Dr. Roderick Macdonald, of Cornwall, Ont., the oldest living graduate of the University; Dr. F. W. Hart, of St. Martinville, La.; Dr. J. J. O'Dea, of Stapleton, Staten Island, N.Y.; Dr. Griffith Evans, India ; Dr. J. D. Macdonald, of Hamilton; Dr. Joshua Chamberlain, of Frelighsburg ; Dr. Temple, of Toronto ; Dr. Burritt, of Toronto; Dr. Hamel, of Quebec; Dr. Markell, of Cloverdale, Cal.; Dr. Shirriff, of Huntingdon, Que.; Dr. Hurd, of Newburyport, Mass.; Dr. Mullin, of Hamilton ; Dr. Gickie, of Toronto ; Dr. Aikens, of Toronto; Dr. I. H. Cameron, of Toronto ; Dr. Fulton, of Toronto ; Dr. Adam Wright, of Toronto ; Dr. Rooney, of Auburn, Cal.; Dr. Ridley, of Hamilton ; Dr. Gun, of Durham, Ont. ; Dr. O'Reilly, of Toronto; Dr. Taylor, President of Bellevue Hospital Med. School, New York ; President Eliot, Harvard University; Dr. Pepper, Provost of the University of Pennsylvania ; Principal Grant, of Queen's College ; President Nelles, of Victoria College, Cobourg ; President Wilson, of Toronto University; Dr. Dupuis, of Kingston, Ont.; Dr. Grinnell, of the University of Vermont; Rev. Dr. Norman, Vice-Chancellor of Bishop's College; Bishop Bond ; Dean Baldwin ; Principal Jack, of the University of New Brunswick; Rev. Mr. Stevenson, of Montreal ; Provost Body, of Trinity College, Toronto; Dr. Hays, of Philadelphia ; Dr. G. C. Shattuck, of Boston; Dr. Shrady, of New York ; Dr. Calvin Ellis, Dean of Harvard Medical Faculty ; Dr. Alf. C. Post, of the University of New York, and others.

The following telegrams were received and sent:—

WOODLANDS, CALIFORNIA.

Congratulations to my Alma Mater; regret I cannot be present.   THOS. ROSS. .

CHICAGO.

The infant sends greeting to the matron. Give mine to the professors and alumni.

LEONARD ST. JOHN,
College of Physicians & Sugeons of Chicago.

To. Dr. St. John,
   College of Physicians and Surgeons, Chicago.

The Matron to the Infant,—May your weaning be safe, your dentition easy, your childhood healthful and your manhood vigorous!

TORONTO.

The Medical Faculty and students of Trinity Medical School send their most cordial greetings and best wishes to the Medical Faculty and students of McGill College on this most auspicious occasion.

WALTER B. GIEKIE,
                Dean.

                                      EDINBURGH.
Congratulations.

ARTHUR D. WEBSTER.

The following message was sent to Dr. Roderick Macdonald, of Cornwall:

The Medical Faculty and graduates celebrating their fiftieth session send their heartfelt and fraternal greeting to Dr. Roderick Macdonald, the oldest living graduate of the University.

THE CHAIRMAN proposed the toast of Her Majesty the Queen, which was duly honored, the band playing "God Save the Queen."

THE CHAIRMAN, in next proposing the health of His Excellency the Governor General, said,—In proposing you the health of His Excellency, I need scarcely say that ever since he has come among us he has identified himself with everything connected with the interests of the country. Perhaps in no respect, however, has he manifested greater interest than in subjects connected with the education of the people. He has, in addition, endeavored to establish amongst us institutions such as those existing in the mother country, and which, no doubt, will be of equal benefit to us. I allude especially to the establishment of the Canadian Academy of Arts, and the Canadian Royal Society. It is only by cultivating the intellectual life among us, that we can hope to take a position alongside our neighbors south of the line 45. We are endeavoring to meet them in the arena of commerce, and we must also endeavor to meet them in the arena of those higher attainments connected with education. We are greatly indebted to our present Governor General for having given an impetus to—nay, for originating—the two societies I have mentioned. We owe him, however, another and a higher tribute of gratitude for having brought amongst us the daughter of our beloved Queen. (Applause). There can be no doubt that the presence of a member of the Royal Family amongst us has tended to strengthen the ties that bind this Dominion to the mother country, has brought us into closer relationship with the people of that country, and made us feel prouder of our origin and more desirous of maintaining our connection with the mother land. In proposing, therefore, the health of the Governor General, we associate with it that of Her Royal Highness the Princess Louise; who, by her own example, has done much to excite in the young ladies of Canada, a love of literature, of art, and of general culture. I am sure you will give this toast an enthusiastic reception.

The toast was duly honored.

Dr. T. L. Brown, of Melbourne, in response to a request of the Chairman, sang a song.

TOAST—THE LIEUTENANT GOVERNOR OF QUEBEC.

THE CHAIRMAN, in proposing the health of his Honor, the Lieutenant Governor of Quebec, said :—The third toast will, I am sure, present itself to every graduate in Medicine of McGill College, with a special recommendation. (Cheers). It is a happy coincident that the representative of Her Majesty in this Province is not only a member of our own profession, but also a graduate of our own University. (Applause). We have the distinguished honor of claiming the Lieutenant Governor as one of our graduates, and as one of his old teachers I may say that it affords me peculiar pleasure to propose this toast, for I had the honor of assisting in his medical education. His Honor the Lieutenant Governor possesses not only a knowledge of medicine, but that breadth of view and interest in social and political questions, conjoined with a liberal education, which are necessary to a statesman. Possessed of such sympathies and views, our colleague early entered public life, and attained a distinguished position in our Canadian House of Commons, having been for some time one of Her Majesty's Ministers. His services to his country and his personal character, deserved the high honor that was conferred upon him when he was selected for the distinguished position he now holds as the representative in his own Province of Her Majesty the Queen. Long may he live to enjoy this honor!

His Honor Lieutenant Governor Robitaille, in responding, said:—

Mr. President and Gentlemen,—The festival that brings us together cannot fail to excite in our hearts feelings of a patriotic joy. True it is, that we have not assembled to commemorate a victory over the enemies of our common country, nor a great political event which has been pompously consigned to the annals of history; but we are commemorating the foundation of a work whose objects and results have been of immense advantage. The foundation of a University is an intellectual victory and a social event, and the opening of the 50th session of one of its most important faculties is a glorious day for society, which has for such a long period benefitted by such victory and social event.

McGill University is the first branch among our Canadian Universities; it has the honor to be chronologically at the head of those superior institutions which are the pride of our Province. (Cheers). Having been founded by Royal Charter in 1821, it only commenced operations in 1827, and after a few years' suspension, it can now reckon fifty years of active work, and in a young country like ours, fifty years, it will be admitted, is a long period of existence, a respectable age. I am aware that several European Universities glory in having to go back to the earliest periods of their national histories to find their origin. Oxford and Cambridge, for instance, appear from the latter end of the first part of the middle ages, like two luminous stars guiding the English nation through the darkness of ages to the extreme limits of intellectual development. (Cheers). But we must not forget that this country of ours sprung into existence at a time when numerous European nations were entering the age of decrepitude. And considering the necessary preliminaries, the long period of formation, the outside battles and the arduous labours required to acclimatise and lay down on a solid basis the social elements, fifty years constitutes a respectable age for a Canadian University. When the foundation of McGill University was laid by that great patriot who gave it his name, and whose memory will be for ever cherished as a benefactor, this country was beginning to feel the want of that rapid development which we all have witnessed since, and it was becoming urgent to provide for a high professional education. The limits of the inhabited part of the Province were rapidly being removed farther back. Canadians were gaining ground over the forest and its solitudes. New townships, new parishes, new towns, villages, and centres were thrown open to settlement, and a number of colleges, seminaries and schools were providing society with a comparatively large number of educated young men. For all these townships, parishes, towns, counties, medical men, lawyers and other professional men were required to help their fellow citizens. At the same time the interests at stake becoming more and more considerable and important, it was necessary to procure a more serious, more scientific, more complete professional education.

McGill University sprang into existence at the proper time to provide for the wants that were felt, and its foundation opened a new era for the development of science in this country. Three large Universities have sprung into existence like so many shining lights—McGill, Laval, and Lennoxville. From the Chairs of those noble and lofty institutions, eloquence, erudition, the medical, legal and philosophical sciences have flowed in abundance, preparing and nourishing the minds of generations of students. From these Universities have gone forth men who have become not only an honor to our Province, but who have reflected credit in foreign lands upon the institutions where they received their training, as you have seen by the letters and telegrams read here to-night. (Cheers.) The diffusion of primary instruction also dates from that period. Throughout the land, thanks to the intelligent initiative of Legislators, to the zeal and energy of the clergy and of a number of devoted citizens, primary schools have been introduced in the different parishes, cities and towns, and this Province enjoys the advantages of one of the best systems of education. The fiftieth anniversary, therefore, is a proud day not only for McGill University, but also for the whole Province. Looking back upon that space of time, the Principal, the Professors, the Directors, the contributors, and the pupils, have every reason to feel proud and thankful that so much good has been accomplished. McGill has contributed its full share to the progress which has been accomplished. Its annals are spotless; its professors are worthy of their high standing—its libraries, museums, and edifices form one of the finest ornaments of this Province. For my part, gentlemen, I feel proud and happy to claim McGill as my *Alma Mater*. (Cheers). It is a pleasing duty for me to proclaim openly my esteem for such an institution. Its degree of M.D. is a passport not only on the continent of America, but also in Europe.

In conclusion, may I be permitted, as a gratification to my feelings, to express my wishes for this noble institution; may its worthy and devoted principal and professors be long spared to diffuse the brilliant light of science and continue to lead it on to success and prosperity; may its libraries, its museums, its edifices increase; and finally, may its *alumni* yet increase in number and keep up its good fame throughout the world. (Loud applause.)

Toast—THE PRINCIPAL OF McGILL UNIVERSITY.

THE CHAIRMAN,—The toast which it is now my honor to propose will, I am sure, be received with not only great enthusiasm but with great affection by every graduate of the McGill College, as well as by every person in the room, who knows anything of the man—it is that of the Principal of the University. (Loud cheers.) It would be quite impossible for me to do anything like justice to this toast, even were I to occupy an indefinite time in the attempt. I will not, therefore, make any such attempt, but will simply recall a few circumstances which will serve in a feeble manner to indicate a small portion of our indebtedness to the Principal. When he arrived amongst us in 1855 and took charge of the University, he found it struggling for existence. In the Faculty of Medicine, however, one of its most important members, it possessed great vitality, while in the other members vitality, medically speaking, was comparatively low. But an era in its history had arrived. A great man had come amongst them and infused new life and

vigor into the institution. If we look broadly at some of the
events in the history of the University since that period, we
shall be able in some manner to appreciate what has been done
under the direction, and mainly owing to the personal efforts,
of its Principal. Thanks to the energy and the efforts which
were put forth by this stranger we find, the year after his
arrival, an endowment fund of $36,440—almost equal to the
original sum left by the founder of the University, Mr. McGill.
In the same year a Chair of English Literature was founded by
the brothers Molson at a very considerable expense—I think
$29,000. All this was in the very first year after Principal
Dawson's arrival, and was the first manifestation of an active
public interest in the University since its existence was secured
by the Medical Faculty. In 1861, six years later, we find,
thanks to the same indefatigable worker, the William Molson
Hall erected, containing our library and public room, together
with the western wing of the main building, in which are our
lecture rooms and museum, being a monument of the liberality
of the late William Molson. (Cheers.) This gift originated
largely in the interest which was now being felt by the citizens of Montreal generally in the work of university education.
It was not that the wealth of the citizens had enormously increased,—it had been great previously—but that larger ideas
had taken possession of our merchants, who began to feel that
there was something better to be done than merely amassing
large fortunes and obtaining honor and reputation as merchants. Ten years later the University makes another
advance. At that time the sum of $26,000 was contributed by
the citizens and the Peter Redpath Chair of Natural Philosophy
and the Logan Chair of Geology were founded, and a considerable sum was raised towards the endowment of the Faculty of
Applied Science. The University was growing, you see; they
had now three organized chairs, with substantial foundations
for them. Almost ever since there has been similar progress, owing mainly to the personal influence of the Principal,
to his constant advocacy of the claims of higher education, and
to the admiration which was gradually being felt for the character of the man and the importance of his work, so that public
opinion was being educated up to the point of giving liberally in
the interests of higher education. And only the other day a citi-

zen of Montreal, as were all the other donors whom I have mentioned, as a final act of grace before leaving his native land for his adopted country, erected that magnificent building in which so many of us were assembled last evening—the Redpath Museum. Now, while I am quite ready to give to these donors all the credit that belongs to them, it must be remembered that most of them possessed these means antecedently to 1856, and the development of a public spirit among the citizens and of a disposition to foster the interests of higher education were largely due to the personal influence of one man.

But it is not to his success in building up the material interests of the University that I would allude just now. I think his claims upon our respect are of a much higher kind; I mean his claims as a man—not as the Principal of the University, not on account of the influence he has exercised on the citizens at large, but his individual character as a man. It is not the possession of a knowledge of many branches of science, nor of rare gifts of genius, nor of personal goodness, that constitute the highest qualities of men, but it is the desire and the power to impart to and excite in others the motives, aspirations and resolves to acquire knowledge to do good and to be useful. (Applause.) That is the highest kind of greatness. Nothing else compares with that, in my humble opinion. It is the power to stimulate a desire in others to live a true and noble life, and at the same time to teach it by precept, example and character, that constitute the highest kind of greatness; and these are qualities which, after a long personal acquaintance with our Principal, I think I may safely say he possesses. It is, gentlemen, on these personal grounds (cheers),—for they are infinitely the highest,—as well as on public grounds for what he has done in building up a great university in this our city, that I ask you to give him a bumper, and to give him a grand reception on this occasion.

The toast was received with great enthusiasm, the applause being again and again renewed.

Principal DAWSON, on rising to respond, said: Mr. Chairman and Gentlemen,—I should rise on this occasion with a feeling of great embarrassment to reply to such a toast as that which has been proposed by the Chairman and honored so highly by the meeting, and especially after the very flattering and complimentary remarks of the Chairman, were it not that there was a certain logical flaw—if the Chairman will permit me to point it out—in his address. It was evident, in the very terms in which he spoke, that most of what he attributed to me was really due to other people, and I would like to say a few words on that particular thesis on this occasion. You must bear in mind that the Principal of McGill University is not that high and mighty official whom in the United States they call President of a University. At best he is only a sort of *primus inter pares*, and he is really a kind of servant of servants of the University, and an administrative officer who has to do with an institution highly democratic in its character, and in which every man is practically his own master. (Laughter.) You find on the calendar that the governing body of the institution is its governors, principal and fellows. You see the principal is packed in between the governors and the fellows. He has to be governed by the governors and advised by the fellows, and I should say he has to be a very "jolly good fellow" among the fellows or he is not likely to get much of his own way. (Laughter.) Now you will understand that it is sometimes no easy matter for the Principal of McGill University to accomplish what he desires to do. He cannot do anything of himself, but he has to do only what he is permitted to do by other people. It has been my good fortune to be connected with this University for about half the time that is celebrated on this occasion, that is to say, something more than twenty-five years. I am fully aware that that period has been twenty-five of its most prosperous years, because the previous years were years of beginning and of struggle, while the twenty-five years during which we have been working together are years in which we have been enjoying a good deal of the fruit consequent on the efforts put forth in the previous period. (Hear, hear.) We must not forget this; still, when I came here in 1855 and looked around on the work I had to do, I found the institution struggling with financial difficulties, but while it presented some discouragements, it also offered grounds of hope. While it was an institution with comparatively few students compared with what it has now, and very much fewer graduates, still it had, perhaps, a firmer hold, comparatively, on the people of Montreal and on the people of

Canada than it has now. There were in it elements of hope, and the grand element of hope at that day was the fact that certain men were connected with it. There was at that time a board of governors of McGill University composed of most remarkable men. When I first became acquainted with them in 1855 I congratulated myself heartily that I had come in contact with such a body of men as were then governors of McGill University Of those men only two remain with us, our Chancellor, Judge Day, and the Hon. Mr. Ferrier, both representative men of that body of great and good men who established McGill University under its new charter at that time. These were men to whom one could go with confidence for advice, men of the strongest public spirit with regard to everything connected with the welfare of this country, who were most earnest in their zeal for education and willing to make great sacrifices for it—who were willing even to run great pecuniary and personal risks for what they believed would bear good educational fruit in the future. With a body of men like these, I do not care if an institution has not a sixpence, it will be sure to succeed (hear, hear), and that was the feeling I had in connection with these men. (Cheers.) I believe it was owing not merely to our founder, Mr. McGill, not merely to the wealthy benefactors of the College, not merely to the citizens of Montreal who have done so much for us, but to the personal influence of these men in calling out the liberality of the citizens, that much of our prosperity is due; indeed I know it to be so. But there were other elements of hope in those days. We were placed here in the midst of a large and wealthy commercial community, to which appeals could confidently be made when it was satisfied that anything could be done which would be of benefit to the community as a whole. Besides, there were at that time, not merely in the Faculty of Medicine but in the Faculty of Arts, able and good teachers well qualified to give a good reputation to the University. I may mention to you the names of Holmes, Campbell, Hall, Bruneau, Crawford, Fraser and Sutherland (cheers), who have now passed away, and I might add the names of our Dean, of Dr. Wright, Dr. Scott and Dr. McCallum, the four survivors of that band of 1855—these were the men that constituted the Medical Faculty, As this is a meeting specially connected

with that Faculty, I may well take the Medical Faculty as
a specimen of the whole, and you can easily understand that
with a body of men like that to uphold a medical school and
make the great sacrifices, even pecuniary sacrifices, that they
did in the interests of their students, there was every prospect
that it would succeed. (Cheers.) And I may say here, in
this connection, that the obligations of the University to the
Medical Faculty are very great. Dr. Howard claimed this in
his address of last evening, and he was right in making the
claim. The men who established the Medical Faculty, who
devoted themselves to it so enthusiastically and so earnestly,
were men who have given character to the University, and
who, by sending out a great body of professional graduates,
and establishing thereby a claim on the gratitude of the country, have done very much to strengthen and promote the other
faculties. But I may say, also, that this influence was reflex.
When I looked at the lists of graduates to-night, I found the
number was very small in the early years of the Medical
Faculty. It took a somewhat rapid start after 1837. Then,
if you look at the graduating classes of 1859 and following
years, you will see a large increase that has been maintained
up to the present day. But you must bear in mind that the
class of 1859 represents the men who entered in 1855 and 1856,
so that the revival in all the faculties at that time doubled the
number of the medical graduates, and thus the medical faculty
itself has enjoyed something of the benefit which the other
faculties have conferred on the University. I speak of these
things because it seems proper to do so on the fiftieth anniversary of the Medical Faculty, and especially when I think
that we older men here to-night cannot possibly survive to
another such anniversary, or even twenty-five years longer.
But when I see all around me these young men, and consider that they are the representatives of all the hundreds of
young men who have gone out as graduates of this University, and when I consider that the most important offices in
the University are being filled by our own graduates, and
that many of the most important offices in the country, from
our Lieutenant-Governor downwards, are being filled by our
graduates (cheers), I know and feel that I and other older
men, when we pass away from the stage, will leave no blank—

that in place of each one of us there will be twenty other and younger men ready to enter upon and carry on the work we have begun. We have seen in the Medical Faculty itself that though the seven men whose names I gave have passed away since I became connected with the University, they have had their places filled by the able men who have come in, so that it stands to-day in as high a position as ever, and is doing more scientific work than ever. Therefore you will understand that we all have grounds for looking forward with confidence to the future of this University, in the belief that, with God's blessing, it is quite certain that fifty years hence it will be fifty times the University that it is to-day. (Applause.)

Toast—Our Sister Colleges.

The Chairman called upon Dr. Wm. Osler, Secretary of the Medical Faculty, to propose the next toast.

Dr. Osler said: I regret exceedingly that owing to the indisposition of Dr. Craik, he cannot be here to propose the toast which we had placed to his name. However, as it has fallen to my lot to replace him on this occasion, I will briefly propose—" Our Sister Colleges."

As the medical profession exists in the interests of the public, and of the public only, it is of the highest importance that our colleges should be so appointed and equipped that they can graduate men well and thoroughly trained. To know how many of these institutions have developed from small beginnings to the high standard which many of them at present occupy, is, in my opinion, the very best training for any one connected with a college, so that each one may be in a better position to do his duty towards his own institution. (Cheers.) There is no better study for a teacher than the way other institutions do their work and the methods they adopt in conducting their classes. During the past eight or ten years it has been my good fortune to be able to do this in some small degree in the institutions on this continent, in Great Britain, and on the continent of Europe, and I am sure that study has done me good. Of certain of these, I am happy to say that we have worthy representatives among us here to-night. (Cheers). We have with us, I am happy to say, from across the line, a representative of Harvard—that University which, above all others on his continent, deserves the thanks of medical men. (Cheers). Though second on the list in the order of seniority, that institution has done more than any other on this continent to uplift the standard of medical education. Anyone who has at heart the interests of medical education, will do well to read the reports of President Elliot for the last eight or ten years, and he will learn that that institution has taken a proper stand and has said : Not the number of graduates, but their quality ; not a superficial training, but a deep, well-grounded education, is what we want for our graduates. If the teachers in other institutions of the United States would study the history of Harvard, they will find there such a record that will induce them to be advocates of that higher medical education which is so much needed. (Cheers.) We have also here to-night a representative from our nearest American neighbour, the medical college at Burlington—President Buckham, of the University of Vermont. (Cheers). We also have with us Dr. Workman, emeritus professor of midwifery in the Toronto school, and Dr. Covernton, representative of Trinity Medical College, Toronto. (Cheers.) We have a representative from Laval University of Montreal, Dr. Rottot. I regret exceedingly we have not also one from Laval of Quebec. We have Dr. D'Orsonnens, representative of Victoria, of Montreal, the oldest—next to that of McGill, I think—medical school in Canada. We have also, in Dr. F. W. Campbell, a representative of Bishop's College. I regret extremely that we have no representative of the new Western College, lately established in London. Wishing them, therefore, every success, I give this toast of " Our Sister Colleges."

The toast was duly honored.

THE CHAIRMAN.—In the order of seniority, I would first call upon Dr. Chadwick, of Harvard University, to reply to this toast. I need scarcely introduce him to you, as he is well known to the profession of Canada. You are all aware what immense strides Harvard has been making in medical education, and education generally, in the last few years. Perhaps no other institution in America, not even excepting our Canadian institutions—and that is a great deal for a Canadian to say—has made such great progress as the sister University of Harvard.

Dr. Chadwick then said—Mr. Chairman and Gentlemen, *alumni* of the Medical Faculty, the very complimentary remarks in reference to me personally, have reminded me of a story. A friend of mine was at Hilton Head during the "late unpleasantness," as we call it, together with the Methodist chaplain of a New York Regiment. One day, the chaplain called the soldiers together to exhort them, and they dropped in, one after another, till about one hundred were present. While earnestly engaged in speaking to them, he noticed that the attention of many was distracted from his remarks, and, suddenly turning about, he saw behind him a little private in a cap with the visor over one ear, and a little black pipe in his mouth, making comic gestures at every remark of the speaker. All at once the chaplain suddenly turned round to him and said, " Well, my fine fellow, I think the Lord will smile on our efforts, don't you? " " Yes," responded the other, " I should think he would snicker right out." (Laughter). Now, gentlemen, I am sure the faculty of Harvard would " snicker right out," if they had heard your Chairman speak as he did of my efforts in connection with that University.

But, speaking seriously, it gives me pleasure to reciprocate the kindly sentiments of your Chairman expressed towards the sister colleges, and especially to tender you congratulations on this day, your fiftieth anniversary. We of the Medical Faculty of Harvard University are looking forward to the celebration of our centennial about six months hence. (Cheers.) The Harvard Medical School, in connection with the University, was founded in 1782 with a faculty of only three members. To-day it numbers among its teachers and instructors fifty-six ; that is to say, it has taken into its fold and made active participants fifty-six men in the city and suburbs of Boston. Age, however, does not always bring wisdom, yet I think that in our old age we have adopted a system which has ultimately proved to be a wise one. In 1871 the Faculty of Harvard, convinced of the poor quality of the instruction, and the insufficiency of the attainments of the graduates from all the medical schools in the United States, decided to inaugurate a new system. That new system consisted, in the first place, in lengthening the term of the yearly session from four to nine months. We also introduced what we borrowed from you, gentlemen—and you deserve great credit for it,—we introduced the examination for admission, which was not required before. (Hear, hear). We also introduced a graded course, which you also have had in a slightly different form, that is, at the end of each year we have an examination on the subjects studied during that year, and at the final examination we only go over the subjects of the final year's study. All the schools in the United States, as you know, have a three years' course; we have adopted, temporarily, a four years' optional course, and I am happy to say that about one-sixth of the students elect to study the four years instead of three. (Hear, hear). In addition to lengthening the course of study and requiring an examination for admission, we also raised the tuition fees from $120 to $200 a year. Now, all this could not be done without great sacrifices. The school at that time, 1871, numbered about three hundred students; it was fully recognized that that number would be largely reduced. If I remember rightly, one hundred students came every year from the provinces, every one of whom stopped when the fees were raised and the course was lengthened to nine months. The scholars fell off from 300 to less than 200 the first year, and to meet that the professors voluntarily accepted one-third of their former salaries, the University stepping in and guaranteeing to them that they should have a salary amounting to about one-third of what they received before. (Hear, hear). The first few years the school was run with a deficit, which was made good by the University, but charged against the medical school. As time went on the number of scholars increased, and as the fees had also been increased, the receipts began to meet the expenditure, and now, I am happy to say, the income is larger than ever it was under the old system. (Hear, hear). Last year, although the professors' salaries had been considerably increased over the small salaries they had agreed to accept, there was a surplus of $7,000. (Cheers). This system is succeeding in several ways. It has succeeded in bringing in better pecuniary returns, which is essential to the continuance of the school; it has succeeded in raising the standard of the graduates by the rigor with which both the preliminary and the concluding examinations are held. About 15 per cent., if I remember rightly, are rejected at the preliminary examination, and about 30 per cent. each year fail to get degrees. The standard is raised, as is shown by the fact that, from having a very small percentage of college graduates in the medical school, at the present time something like 53 per cent. of students in the medical school are college graduates. Finally, by taking this bold step in advance of any other school, the college has strengthened its hold on the respect of the community, as is evidenced by the fact that when this school made two successive appeals for money to erect a new building, they raised $300,000 (cheers), and that building is now nearly ready for occupation.

Now, gentlemen, you can do the same for your school. We convinced our community that our school was determined to raise the standard of medical education and to set an example which other schools should follow, and the community has been ready to support us in the attempt. Everyone of you, gentlemen, must bestir himself for your University, in bringing his private and public influence to bear upon the community. One of the founders of your University has recently died, and it is fitting that a chair should be founded in his name—not necessarily with a large endowment—as has been done in Harvard. Let the name of Dr. George W. Campbell go down to posterity (loud applause) connected with a Chair of Surgery, or Anatomy, and let every one of you here present go to work to accomplish that result. (Loud cheers).

The Chairman,—I call upon Dr. Buckham, President of the University of Vermont, to respond on behalf of that institution.

Dr. Buckham,—Mr. Chairman, I am both happy and proud to respond to this toast, and to present you on this occasion the felicitations of one of the younger and smaller institutions of the United States. I suppose that a medical institution, like any other, loves its neighbors, and we are your nearest neighbors. We have gone through the same experience from poverty to a degree of prosperity, which your Principal has described as having been your lot, and I think that has been the history of pretty nearly every educational institution which has attained to prosperity, whether in this or other countries. I notice that in your enumeration of the first ten medical institutions in the order of seniority, you do not include the University of Vermont. I will not on this occasion dispute the accuracy of that statement, nevertheless, I think we are an older institution than some of those mentioned—I say an older institution, Mr. Chairman, not a better. I was noticing this morning in the Montreal *Herald*, an article entitled " The Future of Montreal." I know something of the past of Montreal, having lived in the province and frequently having been in the city during my boyhood. We have our little art collection at Burlington, and I was noticing in it yesterday a picture of Montreal which I should think was made about seventy-five years ago. It represents a little strip of houses along the river, probably St. Paul and Notre Dame streets, while all the space where the Windsor Hotel now stands was either unoccupied or very sparsely populated. I let my imagination run over this intervening period of seventy-five years. Your population has increased from 12,000 to 150,000. You are spreading over all this island, and when a stranger comes here from the other side of the line and walks your streets, when he beholds your magnificent wharves and warehouses, your streets, and shops and churches, he gets the impression that it is one of the handsomest and, in every way, one of the finest cities on the continent. (Cheers). But it does seem to me—if you will allow me to say so—that there are two splendid opportunities for the citizens of Montreal, which are, as yet, but half improved. I heard, with astonishment, at an educational meeting in St. Johns last winter, that you have no public library. (Hear, hear). Now, a city of the size of Montreal, in the year 1882, without a public library, is an anomaly in our civilization. (Hear, hear). Now, it does not become a stranger to say much on such a point as that, but I have noticed sometimes that when a stranger comes to us and lets a word of advice drop, it is generally more heeded than what can be said by a native. (Hear, hear). But I would like to have it remembered, if nothing else I say or do in Montreal is remembered, when I call the attention of some of these wealthy gentlemen who live in the magnificent palaces that I passed by on your streets to-day, to the fact that the very best means of perpetuating your name and endearing your memory to posterity, is to endow a public library in such a city as this. (Applause). Another matter of fact opportunity which is before the citizens of Montreal is the further endowment of the McGill University. That is a matter on which I have had occasion to think much. It seems to me one of the unaccountable facts in the history of humanity, that medical institutions, as such, have received very little endowment. Even our friend here from Harvard informs me that that old and rich institution has but very slight endowments for its medical department. Now, gentlemen, when I think of it, that strikes me as evidence of very great forbearance on the part of the medical profession. (Hear, hear and laughter). You may take men in their weak moments if you like ; the clergy have not a better opportunity. (Laughter). We have all read in history how, when the clergy found a sinner who was in a weak and dying condition, they knew how to extract money from him for endowments to monasteries and churches. Now, I will not advise physicians to take advantage of the weakness of our poor humanity. I merely suggest to them, as something I know from my own experience, that one of the best curative agencies in the possession of our human nature is a large and handsome donation. I know of the case of a lady in the place where I live who was pronounced by all her physicians to be almost at the point of death from consumption. About then she gave $200,000 to endow a hospital, and shortly afterwards she was examined by a no less distinguished physician than Dr. Bowditch, of Boston, who assured her that she would live twenty years longer. (Laughter). So you can say, on the authority of a gentleman who stands at the head of a University that has a medical department, that the endowment of a hospital or the endowment of a medical chair, is almost a specific for pulmonary diseases (cheers and laughter) ; and generalizing this principle, you may say on the same authority, that moderate donations to the same objects are very good prophylactics. Seriously, gentlemen, the whole problem which we have been considering this evening, especially during the remarks of the distinguished gentleman who has just sat down, the whole problem of the success of medical education seems to hinge upon this, the increasing of the endowments of these departments. Those who instruct in medical institutions should be independent of their fees and should have some freedom from engrossing professional cares, and the same evidence of the respect and confidence of the community which those teaching in other departments enjoy. And when that time comes—and I think it will come—when a medical chair will carry an endowment with it, like any other chair, to sustain its occupant, then this problem will be solved; and whether a professor has five students or five hundred, he can exact as a condition for a degree in his department, that degree of attainment which he thinks the case requires. (Cheers.) Gentlemen, not to detain you any longer, I will close with the sentiment: Liberal endowments of medical schools, the need and the opportunity of the hour; and may McGill University have her full share in this bounty. (Applause).

THE CHAIRMAN,—I would ask Dr. Rottot to reply on behalf of the University of Laval.

DR. ROTTOT,—M. le Président et Messieurs, c'est avec plaisir que je me fais l'interprète des sentiments de mes confrères et de tous ceux qui appartiennent à la Faculté de Médecine de l'Université Laval, en un mot, de tous les Professeurs de l'Université Laval, pour offrir mes plus sincères félicitations à l'Université McGill, à l'occasion de son 50me anniversaire. L'Université Laval, comme toutes les institutions qui se livrent à l'enseignement, qui se livrent au bien de l'humanité, voit avec plaisir les autres institutions marcher dans la voie du progrès, et applaudit de tout cœur à leur succès. Mais non seulement l'Université Laval et les autres institutions doivent applaudir aux succès de l'Université McGill, mais tous les individus de cette province, je puis le dire, quelque soit leur origine, doivent voir avec la glus grande satisfaction les progrès immenses qu'a faits l'Université McGill depuis sa fondation (applaudissements). Nous devons voir, par conséquent, avec la plus grande satisfaction les efforts qu'on a faits pour mettre l'Université McGill sur un pied tel qu'elle soit un honneur, non seulement pour les citoyens anglais de Montréal,

mais encore un honneur pour toute la province. Mais qui sont
ceux que nous devons remercier le plus pour avoir fait un tel
état de choses ? Ce sont d'abord les fondateurs de l'Université
McGill ; ce sont ensuite les individus généreux qui, tour à tour.
sont venus, je puis dire avec tant de patriotisme, pour mettre
l'Université McGill sur un pied tel qu'elle est, comme je viens
de le dire, un honneur pour toute la province. Nous devons
remercier aussi les savants Professeurs que l'Université McGill
a possédés et qu'elle possède encore, car c'est surtout par leur
science qu'ils ont répandu cet éclat que l'on voit briller aujour-
d'hui sur le Collège McGill, et cet éclat que leurs élèves, surtout,
ont su répandre bien loin (applaudissements). Je suis donc
heureux de vous offrir nos plus sincères félicitations, et nous
souhaitons que l'Université McGill marchera de plus en plus
dans la voie du progrès, et nous souhaitons surtout que la
Faculté de Médecine que nous connaissons le mieux, continuera
encore à fournir son contingent de médecins savants et habiles,
comme elle a fait dans le passé, et nous ne doutons pas que
sous l'influence de leur nouveau doyen une nouvelle impulsion
sera donnée à la prospérité et à l'utilité de cette institution
(applaudissements)

The CHAIRMAN—I now call upon Dr. Workman to respond
on behalf of the institution he represents.

Dr. WORKMAN—Mr. Chairman and Gentlemen, Graduates of
McGill,—Unfortunately, the last institution which I have had
the honor of representing was the Asylum for the Insane.
(Laughter.) Perhaps the Chairman has called upon me to
speak in reference to that institution ; if so, I am not at all
ashamed of it. But he may have called upon me from my
connection with the old Toronto School of Medicine, which
was formerly called the Rolph School, having been established
by the Hon. John Rolph, in which I was a lecturer for six or
seven years. I remember the infancy of that school almost as
well as I do that of McGill College. When I look around me
to-night and see all these graduates who have become eminent
men, I feel lost. I can hardly realize my own identity, much
less that of the University. It reminds me of a circumstance
I once read, where a countryman of mine—I suppose it was a
murder case or a shooting case—was called upon to state his
knowledge with regard to a certain gun, and the question was

asked him, "How long had he known that gun?" "Faix," says he, "I have known it ever since it was a pocket-pistol." (Laughter.) And so it is exactly both with regard to the Toronto School of Medicine and McGill College ; as to the former, it has outgrown me altogether,—and as to McGill, I am entirely lost. You, Mr. Chairman, said last night that our professors formerly taught in a wooden building at the corner of Place d'Armes. I beg leave to correct you. You were young at that time—half a century ago. It was a stone building, and I can remember that it had two stores underground. My first acquaintance with it was rather ominous for me. I had just commenced my studies in the office of my old tutor, Dr. Stephenson. It was about the time of the troubles of 1837-'38, and there was considerable difficulty in obtaining subjects in this neighborhood. Our young men had been out one night making a call, and I was taken over beyond the rear of what was then the Bank of Montreal, along Fortification lane, and turned into a cellar or basement below there. There was a quantity of hay there, and presently a fire was made which was necessary to thaw out some material that was there. (Laughter. I was left alone, and soon I perceived facing me a person that I previously knew very well. I do not think there is a gentlemen here old enough to remember him unless it be Mr. Molson—but there was a celebrated character in this city at that time whom, perhaps, the public might remember, his name was Johnny Doyle. Johnny, one night, diluted his water too much with alcohol, and he was picked up frozen to death. Our fellows that night found him, and there he stood staring at me. He had a beautiful set of teeth, and they were just grinning at me. That was the breaking-in I got.

I am very sorry, indeed, that my very highly esteemed old friend, Roderick McDonald, who preceded me in graduation but not in study, is not here to-night. I think a more excellent man I never knew. With regard to what was said last night by you, Mr. Chairman, in reference to my old tutor, Dr. Stephenson, he was well deserving of all the praise you gave him. I knew what his virtues were, and I know what he did for the Medical Faculty in those days. It was quite impossible at that time to induce any other class than our own profession to take the least interest in forwarding the organization of McGill College.

I believe that until the time it was well established no one could be found to take any interest in it, but the moment they found there was money in it, in they came. (Applause.)

The CHAIRMAN next invited Dr. D'Orsonnens to respond on behalf of Victoria College.

VOTRE HONNEUR,

MONSIEUR LE DOYEN,—Messieurs, je remercie les Membres de la Faculté de Médecine de l'Université du Collége McGill, pour l'honneur qu'ils ont fait à l'Ecole de Médecine et de Chirurgie de Montréal, et la preuve d'estime qu'ils lui ont donnée, en m'invitant, comme son Président, pour la représenter à cette belle et grande fête de famille.

Pour ma part, je me suis toujours plu à regarder cette Université comme mon *alma mater*, quoique je ne puisse pas me donner exactement pour un de ses enfants. Je suis venu trop. tôt! En effet, je faisois mes études médicales en 1836-37-38, période pendant laquelle le Collége McGill ne donnoit pas de cours, mais j'avais l'avantage de suivre l'Hôpital-Général et le bureau d'un de ces plus illustres fondateurs, celui du Dr. Stevenson. Comme la loi exigeoit alors cinq années d'étude, avant d'admettre les jeunes gens à l'examen pour la licence, je puis profiter de la réouverture de l'Université en 1839 et 40, pour suivre la session de cette année, à la fin de laquelle je fus admis à la pratique par le Bureau Provincial. Ce sont ces circonstances qui ont fait que je ne suis pas un des gradués du Collége McGill, quoique en réalité je sois véritablement un de ses élèves.

Je puis ajouter même que, dans les premières années de mon professorat à l'Ecole de Médecine et de Chirurgie de Montréal, le regretté Dr. Holmes, m'offrit le diplôme ordinaire de l'Université McGill que, par un excès de susceptibilité peut-être, je, crus alors devoir refuser!

Quoiqu'il en soit, je m'associe de tout cœur à la belle fête d'aujourd'hui pour rendre hommage à la mémoire des Stevenson, des Robertson, des Holmes, des Campbell, ces hommes de cœur, d'intelligence, d'énergies, de dévouement, qui, dans leur patriotisme, pour propager leur vastes connasssances médicales, ont posé les bases solides de cette belle institution et formé, pour continuer leur œuvre, la plupart de ses Professeurs actuels qui, toujours à la tête du progrès, font l'honneur de leur

Faculté, et remplissent si dignement et si avantageusement les devoirs de leur charge, chacun dans sa chaire !

Témoin de ses premiers débuts, j'ai vu grandir avec plaisir et marcher toujours d'un pas gigantesque ce premier collége pour l'éducation médicale dans notre pays. Comme Canadien, je m'énorgueillis de cette belle Université qui jouit déjà d'une réputatation Européenne : comme citoyen de Montréal, je la regarde comme une des gloires de notre cité : comme médecin : je suis heureux de reconnaître chez elle le succès de ses nobles efforts pour la propagation de toutes les sciences, dont la connaissance est si nécessaire à l'exercice consciencieux de notre art.

Un peu plus jeune, mais la plus ancienne après le Collége McGill, vient notre Ecole de Médecine et de Chirurgie de Montréal, qui lui doit la plupart de ses Professeurs.

Aussi, comme conséquence toute naturelle, a-t-on vu les sentiments les plus intimes d'estime et d'amitié régner toujours entre les Professhurs de ces deux institutions, qui, côte à côte, n'ont cessé de travailler à peu près un demie siècle, pour inculquer les connaissances médicales, chacune, aux jeunes gens de sa nationalité.

Pendant quelques années même, il y eut entre ces deux corps une alliance qui fit pour ainsi dire de l'Ecole de Médecine et de Chirurgie de Montréal, le département français de l'Université McGill, puisque les élèves de l'Ecole purent alors obtenir le diplôme de cette Université, en subissant leurs examens devant leurs propres Professeurs et au Collége McGill même. Des circonstances mirent fin à cet heureux arrangement, sans toutefois attirer en rien les bons sentiments de confraternité entre les Professeurs des deux institutions, comme le prouve du reste la réunion de ce soir. Aussi l'Université McGill ne prit-elle aucune part aux lettres et aux combats qui furent dès lors la partage de l'Etat de Médecine et de Chirurgie de Montréal. Mais quelques furent les efforts tentés pour détruire cette dernière, cette guerre n'a fait que la grandir, la faire connaître et apprécier davantage. Aussi voit-elle le nombre de ses élèves augmenter tous les ans ; on le porte déjà à plus de cent trente, dès les premiers jours de cette session.

L'Ecole continuera donc, comme par le passé, à faire tous ses efforts pour se rendre de plus en plus utile à l'approbation canadienne-française, comme le fera le Collége McGill pour les jeunes gens d'origine anglaise; et j'ose me flatter que les Professeur des institutions continueront toujours à entretenir entre eux les mêmes sentiments de considérations mutuelle, d'estime et d'amitié qui ont rendu nos rapports si agréables jusqu'à ce jour. Mais avant de terminer, comme je ne dois pas oublier que cette santé est "*aux Ecoles Sœurs,*" qu'il me soit donc permis de fixer leurs distingués représentants de vouloir bien accepter ici l'expression de vive sympathie de l'Ecole de Médecine et de Chirurgie de Montréal pour chacune d'elles, avec les vœux les plus sincères pour une prospérité toujours croissante et un plein succès dans son enseignement.

The Chairman next called upon Dr. Covernton to respond on behalf of Trinity College, Toronto.

Dr. Covernton—Mr. President and Members of the University of McGill,—It affords me great pleasure to respond to this toast. I have the honor of belonging to an institution less ancient than McGill, but one that equally has at heart the work of thorough and sound teaching, anxious to perform that work with no other rivalry than that of endeavoring to send out each year from its walls graduates who will not only do honor to their Alma Mater at examinations, but discharge the important work confided to them honestly and intelligently. When I first knew anything of McGill and its professors, in 1836, it had only been in operation a few years, but possessed then, as now, most able teachers, devoted to their work, jealous of the reputation of their newly chartered college, and anxious that it should stand high in the estimation of the several British colleges at which they had been taught their profession. Trinity has the same aims and aspirations, and nothing more. We can now boast that in our Dominion we have many Schools of Medicine and Surgery, where the arduous work of teaching is as carefully and efficiently performed as in any institution in Great Britain where the matriculation examination,—excepting at the London University—medical curriculum and practical nature of the examination is calculated to insure as sound a test of proficiency and fitness for practice as can possibly be devised, and, as a consequence of these wise precautions, we find that when our students, after graduating at their several colleges, repair to Europe for the further prosecution of their general studies or for devoting themselves to some speciality, where more abundant opportunities at the large hospitals are furnished in the densely populated cities of Great Britain, France or Germany, the Canadian training has sufficed for putting them on a level with those who from the commencement had been taught at the great schools. (Applause.) As an evidence of the high character of the educational advantages afforded in this country, both general and medical, I might instance the large number of medical men who have worthily filled the highest offices in their several Provinces, as also in the Dominion Government—lieutenant-governors, cabinet ministers, members of Dominion and Provincial parliaments, mayors of cities, etc.; also in our professional ranks men educated in this country at the different schools, many hailing from McGill University, who have been appointed professors in the colleges where they received their education, and whose special fitness for the satisfactory discharge of their duties none would question. (Cheers.) One of your oldest graduates, this evening present, has won for himself not only a Dominion but a European reputation in the specialty he, for many years, was engaged in, and the duties of which he so satisfactorily performed. I refer to my old friend, Dr. Workman.

McGill University has, then, abundant reasons to be satisfied with the career of her graduates for the last fifty years, and I can assure you that from Trinity College there will be no other desire than, if possible, to send out each year a number of young men equal to McGill's list on fair but searching examination. (Applause.)

The CHAIRMAN next called on Dr. F. W. Campbell, Acting Dean of the Medical Faculty of Bishop's College, to respond on behalf of that institution.

Dr. CAMPBELL—As Acting Dean of the Medical Faculty of Bishop's College, it becomes my duty, upon its behalf, to respond to the toast of "The Sister Colleges." I am sure you, Mr. Chairman, regret, as I most certainly do, the absence from the festive board to-night of that venerable gentleman, Dr. David, who, almost from the inception of our school, has so ably filled the position of Dean. That regret is increased, as you well know, by the fact that at this moment he is confined to a bed of suffering, and that ere many weeks, perhaps ere

5

many days, we shall have to mourn his loss. When that time arrives the last link will be broken which now, in this city, binds the present profession to the past. To you, sir, who so well knows his worth, and the deep regret which he feels at his inability to be present, I need hardly say that I feel that I can but feebly represent him. I know, however, that his full and generous heart would have done that which I now do—extend to our friends of the McGill Medical Faculty the hearty congratulations of the Medical Faculty of the University of Bishop's College upon the attainment of their golden wedding. (Cheers.) Between us, I am bound to say, there is the most cordial friendship, and I firmly believe that the spirit of generous rivalry which exists will always continue. We recognize in the Faculty of Medicine of McGill one which was the means of saving to this Province the University which bears its name, and this was an act the value of which is beyond calculation. (Cheers.) Any one who listened to its story as detailed last evening by my friend, Dr. Howard, the newly elected Dean, to whom I tender my congratulations upon his newly acquired honors (hear, hear, and applause long continued), must have felt that the first members of McGill College, amid difficulties such as we can hardly appreciate, founded this medical school in Canada, rendering the country their debtor and making their name as perpetual as the land itself. To me, who sat under Crawford, MacCulloch, Hall, Fraser and Campbell, all of whom have passed to their rest, the details given last evening by Dr. Howard seemed like a dream being retold, and as I mention these names I am sure I recall to many here pleasant and happy days of student life. (Cheers.) It is a pleasure, Mr. Dean, for me to be also here in my personal capacity as a graduate of McGill, and to have the gratification of taking many a hand in mine which I have not had for nearly twenty-five years, and trying to recall features which an equal number of years ago were very familiar to me. This I have enjoyed most thoroughly. To the Faculty of McGill it must, indeed, be gratifying to find so many of their alumni come to celebrate her golden wedding and to renew the friendship and re-attest the obligation which must ever exist between teachers and student. Fifty years is not much in the history of a University, though it forms a large span in the life of an individual. Yet the fifty years has shown that, great as has been the progress of our country, the Faculty of McGill has ever been alive to all that was required to make our city a chief centre of medical education. (Cheers.) Competition is ever an incentive to exertion, and the existence of it in our good city has, in my opinion, done not a little to improve previous means of instruction. One word more, Mr. Dean, and I am done—Bishop's College Faculty of Medicine wishes its sister Faculty of McGill a life as long as the world shall last, with an activity increasing as its age advances. (Loud applause.)

Toast—THE GRADUATES.

THE CHAIRMAN called on Dr. Scott to propose this toast, and on rising he was greeted with long and continued applause.

DR. SCOTT,—Mr. Chairman, it affords me great pleasure to propose this toast, one of the most important of the evening. It is very proper, I think, that to me should have been allotted this pleasing duty on account of my long connection with the University, which dates so far back as 1835. There was soon after an intermission of three years, and before the classes resumed I was requested during the summer of 1837, by the late Dr. Campbell and Dr. Stephenson, to take a petition round to the citizens of Montreal, asking the Governor in Council to grant aid to the Medical Faculty. The grant was obtained and lectures were recommenced in the fall of 1839. There is a gentleman on my left who attended that course of lectures with myself. For forty-three years I have been connected with the University, and for the last thirty-eight years as a teacher in it, being the oldest on the list. It affords me great pleasure to meet on this occasion students whom I have not seen for thirty years. I am glad of the opportunity to meet such a large number of fellow-graduates, and I regret that more have not been able to join us on this occasion. It is satisfactory to find the graduates of McGill College occupying important positions in various parts of the Dominion as well as outside, and we rejoice to welcome here His Honor the Lieutenant Governor, who was a student of mine, and to whom I lectured in 1856. I shall not detain you any longer at this late hour, and would therefore beg to propose the health of our graduates, prosperity and God's blessing.

The toast was duly honored.

Dr. Grant, Ottawa, being called for by many voices, in responding, said :

Although the evening is considerably advanced, and we have already had presented to us on this important and auspicious occasion, so many interesting topics connected with our institution, still, as one of the graduates of this time-honored College, I can assure you it affords me very great pleasure to have this opportunity extended to me of offering a very few observations. Fifty years have now elapsed since its organization, and although the foundations have only been placed within the last half century, I think every Canadian throughout the length and breadth of this Dominion, has reason to feel proud of what has been accomplished. (Cheers). As an evidence of the prosperity which has attended the efforts of those gentlemen charged with the practical working of this institution, I would ask you to look around the festive table to-night and see the distinguished men who have grown up in our midst, educated at our *alma mater*, and who are now guiding and guarding the interests of the people throughout the length and breadth of this country. Although but a few years have elapsed since the inauguration of the Medical Faculty, what do we find? That this institution is not only recognized in Canada, but in Great Britain and in almost every country in the world, and to-day we can point to our graduates holding distinguished positions in various departments in almost every clime. In the army, in the navy, over hospitals, and other institutions requiring a medical training, we find the pupils and graduates from this University. Is such not an evidence of the prosperity that has so far attended our endeavors? Again, I may say that this reunion brings together old friends parted for many a year. I have met faces since I came here to-night that I had not seen since the day of my graduation in 1854,—and I may say that it is desirable that we, as medical men, should have these reunions frequently, that we might come together and see what time is doing for us, and in the cause of science to see what we can do towards the advancement of our *alma mater*. (Loud applause). I may say also that it is a source of pride and gratification to us all that we have at the head of our institution a man who is looked upon as one of the greatest scientists of the present day, Dr. Dawson. (Great applause). He is known in every country as a man who has established a parallelism between science and religion, who has shown that science, instead of being opposed to religion, is the very foundation on which it rests. (Loud cheers). Then what do we find here to-night? The recently appointed head of the Medical Faculty, Dr. Howard, is one of your own men who has grown up in your midst, whom you have known since boyhood, whom now you esteem worthy to be your Dean, and I will say, Long may he be spared to guard the interests of those who may come under his charge. (Loud cheers.)

We, as medical men, have an important duty to perform, and I trust you will excuse me if I advert to a question which I think demands the serious attention of medical men, and it is that of mental hygiene. Any ordinary observer who will watch the physical and intellectual development of the rising generation, cannot fail to notice an increase in nervous and various other diseases that are sapping the mental vitality of our youth, and it is highly important that we as a medical profession should firmly insist on the importance of the great evil of cramming and the over-storing of that tender mind and that poor little brain. We see children going to school in these days with more books under their arms than they can carry. (Cheers). There is danger that, in this new country of ours, where education is so general, the brain will be over-burdened, and that a generation is growing up that will not be able to accomplish what the times will demand. (Cheers). To my mind, this is one of the most important questions of the day, and I hope that every physician will find time to look into it, and to impart such teaching to parents that we may raise up a generation in this country that will be both practical and useful. I do not desire to detain you longer. Suffice it to say that as a graduate of McGill University, I have very great pleasure in being here to meet so many of my old friends, and I feel proud and happy that so much prosperity has attended the endeavors of those in charge, and I trust that many around this festive board will be present at the centennial anniversary. (Loud cheers).

Toast—SISTER PROFESSIONS.

DR. HINGSTON, being called upon by the Chairman to propose this toast, said : Mr. Chairman and gentlemen, to propose a toast such as this is a duty that belongs of right to the chair or one of the vice-chairs. However, I am glad of the opportunity it gives me of expressing the great pleasure I have in meeting with you all here to-night on an occasion that can hardly come twice in the lifetime of any individual. Although Dr. Grant seems to look forward to such an event for some, in all human probability there will not be many of us present on that far-off occasion. It is pleasant to meet our old fellow-students, and it is to me a matter of exquisite pleasure to shake hands again with fellow graduates of thirty years ago. I was pleased that some of them recollected me and that I recollected them, notwithstanding the changes which time has made. Yet there is necessarily an element of sadness in such meetings—to shake hands in middle age or advanced years with those whom we met in our younger days when full of health and strength and vigor, and now again after the lapse of years with feelings, perhaps, very much changed. But as in the physical world there is a correlation of forces, so also is there a correlation of forces in the mental and moral worlds. Of trials, and sufferings, and anxieties of mind each one has doubtless had his share during those intervening years. And these are forces not to be lost, but which have their correlative value in sympathy. Fortunate would it be for us and for them if our sympathies for our fellow-creatures have increased in proportion to the trials and anxieties we have experienced in the past. And now, gentlemen, permit me to say a word to the Dean. Mr. Dean, I wish to express the intense pleasure I have in styling you, my old personal friend and fellow-student, Dean of the Faculty of Medicine. (Applause.) I wish, Sir, you had told me whether I should limit myself to certain professions in this toast, or whether I should take in all those that wish to be styled the sister professions. They are now becoming so very numerous that it is altogether impossible to enumerate and define them. There is the tonsorial profession, for instance; there is the profession of dentine, enamel, and cementum attached to our profession; there is the chiropodical; and, between this, the plantar pedis—where I shall end—to the

vertex capitis—where I began, so many segments of learning
are met with, that titles appropriate to the professors in each
segregated portion are difficult of coinage. However, I think
I shall not depart from the good old custom, but propose the
toast to the three learned professions—divinity, law and medicine. That is the order now-a-days, but not the order which
would have been observed two hundred and fifty years ago. It
is, Mr. Chairman, a matter of Canadian history that long after
doctors were here in great numbers, and fattened in the land,
there was no such thing as a lawyer. (Laughter.) There was a
long period in the early history of Canada during which it
was considered right and proper and necessary that surgeons
should dwell among the colonists; but unwise to allow a lawyer
to put his foot upon the soil of Canada. (Hear, hear.) In
looking over old papers we find numerous names of men who
were styled *Churigien du Roi*, but we do not find the name
of a single lawyer. L'Escarbot, at a later period, was permitted by the government of France to come here *alone;* but,
as you may well imagine, he was not very happy. There was
no other lawyer to dispute with him as to the law of *meum*
and *teum*, and to establish that nice division of estates between
lawyer and client. (Laughter.) But it was a fact that for a
long period no lawyer was allowed to set his foot on the virgin
soil of Canada. What a change since then! and I dare say it
will be pretended we are very much better for the change. As
to the professors of divinity, it would ill become me to speak
in the same vein. We seek, as Cowper did, "that divine sim-
plicity in him who handles things divine." Of course we
always find it. (Laughter.) As to our own profession, it
speaks through the tongues of those who, grateful or ungrateful, unceasingly bestow on their physician so generous a meed
of censure or of praise. With these observations, Mr. Dean, I
shall propose the Sister Professions in the limited sense—the
professions of divinity, medicine and law.

Rev. Prof. Murray being called upon by the Chairman to
respond on behalf of divinity, said:—Mr. Chairman and Gentlemen,—In rising to respond for the profession of divinity I
beg to state, at the outset, that I do so merely as a sort of
make-shift. I was approached by one of the Committee connected with the arrangements for this evening, who told me

that all the clergy who had been invited to the banquet had
declined, and that they must, therefore, depend on me for
representing that profession. Now I feel as if I were intrud-
ing into a position to which I have no very just claim when I
take it upon myself to speak for the ministerial profession. It
is true that I was educated for that profession, but I have never
occupied any position in connection with it, having been,
almost immediately after leaving college, called to a position
as professor. At the same time, I need scarcely say that I
can never fail to retain an interest in those studies with a view
to which I was brought up in my early life, and I make this
remark all the more upon the present occasion because it leads
me to say that the theologian is one who, by the very nature
of his calling, by the very nature of the sciences which he is
called to study, takes an interest at the same time in nearly
every branch of human knowledge, and especially in those
branches over which the Medical Faculty of a university pre-
sides. It is said that too many clergymen treat man as if he
were all soul and no body. Well, I need scarcely remind you
that the opposite charge has sometimes been brought against
you, gentlemen, of treating man as if he were all body and no
soul. I think you will justify me in saying that no philosophical medical practitioner could take such a view of that marvellous nature which it is his duty to treat in case of disease;
I think he will admit that medical practice compels him to
recognize something more than a mere animal nature in man,
compels him to recognize the fact that man is endowed with
an imagination that broods over the past and tortures him
with forebodings of the future, with a knowledge whose
thoughts wander through eternity, and that this mental nature
is constantly liable to various diseases. I was glad to hear Dr.
Grant refer to that in the exceedingly able remarks he made a
few moments ago. Those remarks, I think, will convince
anyone that the medical practitioner is forced to recognize the
fact of the mental life of man as well as his bodily or animal
life, and that the sources of disease are often developed and
encouraged from ignoring these circumstances. In the same
way I do not hesitate to acknowledge that no philosophical
clergyman, no clergyman who thoroughly realizes the duties
he is called to perform, can overlook the fact that man is not

merely a spiritual being, but a spiritual being who requires an animal organism to work out the duties to which he is called in life by his Maker, and that the perfection with which we perform those duties depends upon our keeping this animal organism with which we are endowed in the highest state of efficiency of which it is capable. The clergyman, if he is faithful to his duties, will therefore endeavor to impress upon those with whom he has to deal, that they are unfaithful to the trust which God has given them in the world, and unfaithful to that marvellous physical organism with which they have been endowed, if they do not treasure it so as to make it as efficient an instrument as possible of performing the work which they are called upon to do. I find, indeed, gentlemen, in a motto which has been attached to this toast, that those who have drawn up the programme of the evening have, while making reference to the professions, adopted the function of the clergyman in enjoining the duties of life which the clergyman is supposed to enjoin, for we are here informed that the best physic that even a doctor can prescribe is the virtue of temperance. Well, the lawyer is turned into a preacher too by being told that the best law he can give to his clients is a patient disposition of mind. But I am glad also to find that the clergyman is reminded that a good conscience is the best divinity. (Cheers.) But I find that temperance is here put at the head of the virtues, and I wish to practice that virtue on the present occasion. I wish to cultivate temperance in speech, not that I have any temptation at the present moment to be intemperate in the sense of using any improper language. I think that total abstinence is best in regard to that. But I wish to practice the virtue of temperance in the length of my remarks, and I shall therefore conclude by expressing the belief and the hope that the medical profession will find in the more intelligent members of the clerical profession zealous helpers in the work which they are called to do, by the clergymen preaching what I consider to be a very wise gospel—the gospel of devout submission to the will of God as it is manifested in the laws of the animal organism with which we are endowed. (Cheers.)

Mr. W. H. KERR, Q.C., Dean of the Faculty of Law, being called upon by the Chairman to respond on behalf of the Bar, said:—Mr. Chairman and Gentlemen,—In rising to respond to the toast concerning my own profession, I feel my inability at this hour of the night to do justice to it, not only from my own want of power but also from the want of time. The three learned professions of divinity, law and medicine—though I may change the order in which Dr. Ilingston gave them—march in the van of the army of civilization. To them are to be ascribed nearly all the great deeds that adorn history, and in the future, as in the past, it is to be hoped the profession of which I have the honor to be a member will always advocate right and protest against wrong, and, if necessary, make any sacrifices to accomplish its objects.

On this glorious occasion, however, even as there is no pleasure unalloyed, there is a drop of bitterness in the sweet cup that is offered us—I allude to the loss which the Medical Faculty has recently suffered through the death of the late lamented Dean. His generosity and his kindness endeared him to all, whilst his pre-eminent talents as a surgeon adorned the Chair which he occupied in this University. (Applause.) The fragrance of his memory will long endure, and will call back to us, his fellow students, the loss which we have all suffered by his death. Gentlemen, as one of the mottos of our profession is that brevity is the soul of wit, I merely wish, on behalf of the profession of law which I am called to represent, and of the Faculty of which I have the honor of being Dean in the University, all success, honor and prosperity to the Faculty of Medicine. (Cheers.) May the members of that Faculty all walk in the path of duty; and when fifty years more shall have elapsed and your successors, gentlemen, celebrate its centenary, may all men throughout the length and breadth of the land then say:— those who established McGill University. and those who labored to maintain it in years of trouble and discouragement, have deserved well of their countrymen. (Applause.)

The CHAIRMAN—Before the next toast on the list is proposed I would like to make a very gratifying announcement to the graduates in Medicine here assembled and to the friends of the University. I hold in my hand a letter, the writer of which has earnestly requested that his name shall not be given now, or for some time to come. It is the first fruits, I think, of the appeal which I humbly made last evening on behalf of the profession of medicine to which I belong, and I cannot help thinking that the citizens of Montreal will take the same view as the writer of the letter I am now about to read :—

"My Dear Howard,—The remarks in your admirable address of last evening, on the necessity for increased means to enable you to extend and render still more efficient the work of your Faculty, impressed me so strongly that I shall be glad to assist in procuring this, and now make the proposition that if, by the 1st of August next, you succeed in securing the $50,000 referred to as the Campbell Memorial Fund, I shall have the pleasure of handing you an additional $50,000 for the purposes of the Medical Faculty of McGill University. You may, if you please, say so at your dinner this evening, withholding my name, which I do not wish to be known in connection with it, at least until you can exact from me this promise, and this doubtless the well known liberality of your fellow-citizens will enable you to do."

Prolonged applause followed the reading of this letter.

Toast—THE FOUR FOUNDERS.

Principal DAWSON—There is another toast without which this meeting would not be complete, the toast to the four founders of the Medical Faculty. We should, gentlemen, always remember with honor and gratitude the men who are the founders of any good thing. It is easy for men to follow after others have shown the way. It is difficult to begin a good thing which has not been done before, and the men who founded the first medical school in the Dominion of Canada deserve to be held in everlasting remembrance. Three of these men I had not the pleasure of knowing personally, Drs. Stephenson, Robertson and Caldwell; the fourth, Dr. Holmes, I did know, and esteemed and loved him. He was Dean of the Medical Faculty when I came to Montreal, and I have not met any man more deserving of respect and love. He was not only eminent in his profession but he was an eminent Christian man, most public-spirited, an accomplished botanist and mineralogist, whose collections now adorn our museum, and who, until the last, took an earnest and lively interest in every matter that concerned the welfare of his fellow men and the pro-gross and advancement of humanity. I believe the other three men must have been like him. I propose, therefore, the "Four Founders of the Medical Faculty of McGill University." I ask you to drink this toast in silence, with a prayer that the good work which these men began may continue to prosper, and that we may be able to follow worthily in their footsteps.

The toast was drank in silence.

Toast—THE MONTREAL GENERAL HOSPITAL.

Dr. McCALLUM, being called upon by the Chairman to propose this toast, said :—

The toast I have to propose is one to which I am certain you will all most cordially respond. Ungrateful, indeed, would be any graduate in Medicine of McGill University who would, at any time or under any circumstances, fail to do honor to that noble institution which has furnished him the opportunities of acquiring a practical knowledge of his professsion—*the Montreal General Hospital.* The noble edifices, erected and set apart for the reception of the homeless and friendless sick, which are now found in nearly every town and city throughout civilization, are in the highest degree creditable to our common humanity, and may be regarded as so many monuments of the philanthropic spirit of the age in which we live. Hospitals and infirmaries were unknown to the ancients. Egypt had her magnificent mausoleums for the reception of the dead, and carried to perfection the art of embalming the bodies of the departed. Greece and pagan Rome embellished their cities with stately structures dedicated to the worship of their deities and to the gratification of the senses, the architectural beauties of which, even as exhibited in their ruins, have commanded the admiration of all succeeding ages. Their sages and philosophers reasoned astutely on the nature and destinies of man, and occasionally inculcated sublime lessons of virtue ; but we search in vain in their writings for these higher teachings which place man in his proper relations to his fellows ; nor do we detect the influence of such teachings on their mind in their public buildings. No edifice, unpretending or otherwise, for the shelter of the helpless victim of disease can be discerned amid the profusion of temples and palaces—no asylum for the aged, decrepid or weak. To the humanizing influences of Christianity alone are we, in modern times, indebted for this sight. To the revolution effected in our natural feelings by her pure, unselfish feelings must we attribute the pleasure we experience in the erection and sustentation of various charitable institutions.

The Montreal General Hospital was established in the year 1819. On the first day of May of that year it was opened for the reception of patients. The first building secured for the purposes of the charity was on Craig street. It contained three wards capable of accommodating twenty-four patients. The warm interest which the citizens of Montreal have taken in the welfare of this institution from its inception to the present time, soon led to an active movement to provide for it more ample and suitable accommodation. The result was that the site of the present hospital buildings was secured, and the foundation stone of the central building laid on the 6th June, 1821. The Richardson wing was added in the year 1832, and later the Reid wing and the Morland extension. The General Hospital now contains fifteen wards, capable of containing one hundred and fifty patients.

Shortly after the main building was erected the physicians on the visiting staff, Drs. Stephenson, Holmes, Caldwell and Robertson, associated themselves together for the purpose of establishing a school of medicine, and utilizing the means afforded by the wards of the Hospital for instructing students of Medicine in the practical part of their profession. This organization was the germ of the Medical Faculty of McGill University. Since that time the Faculty and the Hospital have been intimately associated, and by the labors of a succession of earnest, able men the Hospital now enjoys not only a home but an American and a European reputation as a distinguished and successful School of Clinical Medicine and Surgery. I address an audience conversant with the facts, and I have no hesitation in asserting that, to the medical student honestly desirous of preparing himself for the practice of his profession, the Montreal General Hospital has always offered, and now especially offers, a field for the necessary training second to no other on this continent. A distinctive feature of this charity, and one that commends itself to every liberal-minded man, is its catholicity. It is truly a *general* hospital. The nationality, religion or creed of the applicant for admission to its wards receives not the slightest consideration. The only claim recognised, the sole key that opens its portals, is diseased and suffering humanity. If the position and worth of an institution, and its claims on the affection and support of a community, are to be determined by the amount of unselfish good that it has been the means of accomplishing, then, amongst the institutions of Montreal this grand old charity should stand *facile princeps*. I ask you to join me in drinking to the continued and increased success and prosperity of the Montreal General Hospital.

Dr. HENDERSON, upon invitation of the Chairman, sang a song.

The CHAIRMAN—The Treasurer of the Montreal General Hospital, Mr. Davidson, will kindly respond to Dr. McCallum's toast.

Mr. THOS. DAVIDSON—I regret extremely that the President of the Montreal General Hospital has been obliged to leave, and I, a very junior member of the Managing Committee, am left to respond to this toast. I think this may well be termed the toast of the programme, and well deserving of honor, because I think most of the distinguished men of Montreal, ever since the institution was founded, have served upon the Management or in some official capacity connected with it. It has, in fact, had a history of "honor and renown." As was well remarked by the gentleman who proposed the toast, the object of the institution is very fitly expressed by its name—the Montreal General Hospital. Its intimate connection with the Medical Faculty is patent to all. I believe the very founders of the Faculty were the first Medical Board of the Hospital. I need not say anything about the charity itself. It is well known to all the citizens of Montreal who, for many long years, have generously come forward in support of it with subscriptions and donations. There has been no stint in the liberality of the citizens towards this charity. When called upon they have responded nobly; and while liberal to a degree in the past, still, I think that in the future the grave interests of the institution will render it necessary to appeal even more strongly to their feelings. It is clear that if the Medical Faculty is to advance, the Montreal General Hospital must advance in an equal degree. At the present time the Managing Committee are painfully impressed with the fact that the buildings are utterly inadequate, and steps will soon have to be taken to erect a building sufficient for the requirements of the city. Mr. Chairman, I have no doubt the citizens of Montreal will nobly respond to any appeal that may be made to them in that behalf. One eloquent speaker who preceded me to-night suggested a memorial chair to the late Dr. Campbell; in the same way, I think, this would be a good opportunity to get some one to give $200,000 for the erection of a new wing to the Montreal General Hospital. Mr. Chairman, I have to thank the gentlemen present, on behalf of the Committee of Management, for the kind manner in which they have honored this toast. (Cheers.)

Toast—The Medical Faculty of McGill University.

Dr. Grant,—The very important duty now devolves upon me of proposing the toast to the Medical Faculty of McGill College. That faculty is but a contingent of the Grand Army of 180,000 medical men throughout the world, which is supplied to-day with the pabulum of medical thought, in the form of a library, numbering over 120,000 volumes, not including pamphlets on various medical subjects. While I listened to the admirable address of the Lieutenant Governor of Quebec, it occurred to my mind that while, as Canadians, we had pleasure in recognizing the important part our brethren of the French nationality had taken in the development of this country, we as members of the Anglo-Saxon family were pleased to note, that at the present day, the French element is producing the greatest amount of medical literature, and next in order comes the German. Of the 180,000 medical men, only about 12,000 are workers in the path of medical literature for the rising generation. I hope that every graduate of McGill University will bear in remembrance this fact, and that those who have cases presenting any peculiarity, or otherwise, will record the data in the medical journals of our country, and thus in time form a literature, which will give an additional status to the medical profession of our Dominion. Without dwelling on this point, I desire to say that I have very great pleasure in pro-

posing, on behalf of the medical profession, the health and prosperity of the Medical Faculty of McGill University. (Cheers.)
The toast was duly honored.

THE CHAIRMAN,—Gentlemen, on behalf of the Medical Faculty of McGill College, I return you my most cordial thanks for the handsome manner in which you have received the toast which my friend, Dr. Grant, so enthusiastically proposed.

As a Faculty, we have been doing all that we could in the interests of medical education. I think all the members of the several Faculties in the City are doing the same. We can claim the honour of being first in the field. We are the oldest, and we are, perhaps, the largest, and as the oldest ought to have grown the most. I can promise that the present Faculty will do its utmost to maintain the prestige of the past.

It was with feelings of inexpressible delight when, on returning home last evening, I found on my hall table the note which I read to you to-night. That note comes from a friend of the late Dean, and a personal friend of myself, a kind gentleman and a very modest man in everything he does, and with a large, warm Scotch heart. (Hear, hear.) I would like to impress upon you members of McGill College and citizens of Montreal, that we have an opportunity now offered us of creating a fund much needed by our Faculty. The promise of this $50,000 is so sincere and so reliable, that I should not care for the endorsation of the Bank of Montreal on the note. So it rests now with the friends of McGill, and the citizens of Montreal who ought to be friends of McGill—for I maintain that the highest interest of the citizens are the interests that group around that University. The great material interests of the country will always be looked after ; the very selfishness of men will secure that. But it is a singular thing that they are not so apt to be interested in the subject of education, and stranger still, they are less apt to be so in medical education than any other. Why it is that men are more considerate about their fortunes than about their persons, I never could comprehend, but so it is. If men's property is at stake they will spare no pains to protect it, but men frequently hesitate to give a thousand dollars to help to build an institution for the education of a class of men capable of looking after their bodily health. It is an anomaly, and I suppose it arises from this peculiarity in our nature, that the present only engages our attention, and that we are usually indifferent to our health until it breaks down. The impression I want to leave on your minds as graduates and as citizens—and I regret the toast which elicited these remarks did not come in earlier— the impression is this: that the citizens of Montreal owe something to the Medical Faculty of McGill College. If Montreal claims to be the first city in the Dominion in wealth and population, and in all the other interests which belong to a metropolitan city, it seems to me that the citizens should see to it, that its chief educational institution is placed on a footing commensurate with the importance of the city. On this ground I appeal to the citizens of Montreal, and to the mercantile men especially—for they hold the purse-strings, as you know—to come forward and meet the liberal offer of this friend of ours. I ask the citizens at once to form a committee, in co-operation with our Faculty, to collect $50,000, in order that by next August, as we are limited to that time, we shall be in a position to claim from our friend the $50,000 he has promised. Had we a fund of $100,000 from which we could receive a revenue, there are many things we could do in our own Faculty that we are unable to perform. In my lengthy lecture last night I alluded specially to one, and that one Chair I am very anxious to see established. It is quite plain that before long it will become absolutely necessary in the teaching of the several branches of medicine, to have men who deserve the name of experts, who shall devote their time exclusively to teaching certain scientific parts of medicine, and who shall not be embarrassed with the necessity of practising the art. (Hear, hear). There is no question that we must have a person exclusively devoted to chemistry, who shall be a recognized authority in that science, and who shall not be obliged to waste his time and energies by attending to the exigencies of practice. Another necessity, I think, especially if we wish to maintain our present proud position of being the leading medical school in this city and Dominion, is to have also a person who shall be able to devote his time exclusively to physiology, and especially to that department of it which applies to pathology. Original investigation we must aim at. We have men in our province well qualified to undertake such duties, and we should have a chair endowed exclusively for that purpose, as an *appanage* of the University. I ventured to suggest last night, although a departure from what has hitherto been done, so far as I know, in any medical school, the establishment of a chair for comparative pathology. I consider this would be a great step in advance. If there is progress to be made in the science of disease, it must come now largely from the study of disease as a whole, not alone as it is found in man, but as it occurs in the animal and in the vegetable kingdoms. We cannot possibly get a competent man for that position unless we have the means to pay him handsomely. When you recollect the difficulties of mastering the subject of human pathology, and when you add the necessity of a knowledge of general animal pathology, and of the cognate department of vegetable pathology, you will understand that to procure a man versed in those subjects, we must be prepared to pay a sufficient salary. The advantages that would result, not alone to our school, but to the science of medicine in general and to this country, would be so great, that I am satisfied the founder of such a chair would feel amply rewarded. In the name of the Faculty, I thank the gentleman who proposed this toast.

In conclusion, I ask you all, graduates and citizens, to co-operate in this enterprise which we as a Faculty are about to undertake, so that before the first of August next, I should say before three months, we may raise the $50,000 required to secure this munificent offer of a friend. (Cheers).

Toast—The Ladies.

Dr. MacDonnell proposed the toast of the Ladies, accompanying it with the sentiment, " Bibamus salutem earum, et confusionem ad omnes bacularios."

The toast was duly honored.

Toast—The Pharmaceutical Association ; Scientific Pharmacy, the handmaid of Medicine.

The Chairman,—This toast was handed to me by a valued friend, and I am sure it will be most acceptable to this body. The Pharmaceutical profession is so closely linked to our own, that anything which concerns its interests vitally affects the interests of our profession. As it is our handmaid, or right hand, so to speak, I am quite sure our feelings towards it are those of the warmest sympathy.

The toast was duly honored.

DR. GURD,—I beg to thank you, Mr. Chairman and gentlemen, for the toast you have drunk. I have been a member of the Pharmaceutical Association from the beginning, and have been very familiar with the profession for about thirteen years. On behalf of the Association, I thank you for the honor you have done us, and regret that the President, Mr. Manson, had to leave before this toast was proposed.

SHERIFF CHAUVEAU,—I propose a double toast, one to our worthy Chairman, Dr. Howard, and one to our next meeting fifty years hence.

The toast was duly honored.

DR. COPELAND, Chicago,—On behalf of the visiting graduates, I propose a toast to the resident physicians, for their kindness to myself and others on our visit to Montreal on this auspicious occasion.

The toast was duly honored.

The Chairman left the chair at ten minutes past one o'clock in the morning, and the company dispersed.